MAKING A KILLING ON WALL STREET

A TANNER NOVEL - BOOK 3

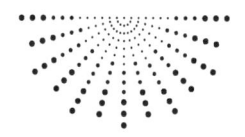

REMINGTON KANE

INTRODUCTION

Tanner's war with The Conglomerate heats up but also grows more complicated as he becomes embroiled in a power struggle within the Calvino Crime Family.

Sophia Verona, daughter of slain mobster Jackie Verona, is in the middle of the conflict and only Tanner can save her, but first, he has to keep himself alive.

Meanwhile, Conglomerate boss Frank Richards has plans to gain more power, while his former assistant Al Trent grows closer to learning the truth about Tanner's "death."

Can Tanner survive and start a new life, or will fate snatch away victory at the last instant?

1
TWO ARE BETTER THAN ONE

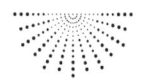

When Tanner spotted the beer mug coming at him from the corner of his eye, he ducked, while also thrusting a fist to the right and punching his attacker in the balls.

That's when the man's four friends decided to join the fight.

Tanner was in rural Pennsylvania in the small town of Ridge Creek, and near the farm he'd been living at with Tim and Madison.

Tanner hadn't been with a woman since he was in Florida nearly a month earlier and after a week on the farm, he was beginning to stare longingly at Madison, he knew it was past time he got laid.

Hell, he was so horny that even Tim was starting to look good to him, so he went to the local watering hole; a big rambling dump named Grover's Bar & Grill that had once been a barn.

It was late afternoon and people were just getting off work, so the bar only held a little more than two dozen patrons, many of which were couples.

Tanner found the pickings slim the first hour he was there and was talking up the middle-aged, but still tasty, bartender, when a pair of women walked in who were young, hot and wearing short dresses that showed lots of cleavage.

One of them was a blonde with huge blue eyes and hair that hung down to her ass. The other was a brunette with shoulder-length hair, large breasts and green eyes that seemed to sparkle.

Tanner zeroed in on them immediately, as did the group of five guys that looked like factory workers. The men wore matching green shirts that had CRAMER STEEL stitched on the back.

The factory workers were closer to the women's table and one of them, a man with a goatee and ponytail, sauntered over there first, but Tanner made a point of catching the eye of the blonde as he leaned back against the bar.

The woman smiled, looked him over, then whispered something in her friend's ear. When the brunette's eyes wandered over him and she licked her lips, Tanner knew his chances had improved. He planned to exit the bar that night with one of the ladies on his arm.

The man at the table followed their gaze, then glared at Tanner and asked him what the fuck he was looking at.

Tanner ignored the man, walked over to the table, and spoke to the women in hopes of leaving with the blonde.

Not fond of being ignored, the ponytailed man sitting with the women stood and told Tanner that he should go back to the bar, "...if he knew what was good for him."

Tanner did know what was good for him, and it was the 108 pounds of primo blonde tail who was seated in front of him and making his cock twitch.

Tanner finally acknowledged the man with a glance, told him to fuck off, and that's when the man swung the beer mug at his head.

As beer mug's four friends charged at him from their table, Tanner stepped atop a chair, leapt toward them and landed in their midst, while smashing two of them against the side of the head with his elbows. The twin blows buckled the men's knees while stunning them, and cut their numbers in half.

The bigger of the two remaining men swung a punch at Tanner that he managed to duck just barely, to then rise and jab his rigid fingers into the man's throat. A second later, the remaining man struck him in the left kidney, making him wince from the pain.

The blow had also knocked the wind out of him, and as Tanner tried to regain his breath, the man swung again and gave him a solid blow above the right eye.

Tanner let out a loud moan, dropped to one knee, and pretended to appear dazed by the blow.

The man grinned down at him, cocked his right fist way back behind his shoulder, and prepared to finish Tanner off with one mighty blow.

This left the man's midsection exposed, and Tanner rose in a flash and buried a knee into it. When the man doubled over, Tanner straightened him up with a forearm beneath the chin and the man fell to the floor of the bar, where he lay flat on his back.

However, the man's friends were all recovering their wits and would be looking to start the battle again within seconds.

When the hand touched his shoulder, Tanner nearly reacted with violence, but the delicate nature of the fingers upon him spoke of their owner before he turned and confirmed it with his eyes.

It was the blonde with the long hair, and when he turned to face her, she placed a caressing hand on his cheek and smiled.

"Let's get out of here."

Tanner nodded, then the other woman joined them as they reached the door.

They were driving away in Tanner's pickup truck when the five guys came stumbling out of the bar shouting curses.

The blonde touched the bruise forming above Tanner's eye. "Does that hurt?"

"Not when you touch it."

"I'm Brittany, she's Amber, and what's your name?"

"Call me, Romeo."

"Romeo? I like the sound of that. Take the next exit and turn right, our apartment is a few blocks down that street."

"You two live together?"

Amber reached across Brittany and rubbed Tanner's chest.

"We do everything together."

Tanner smiled. He had hoped to leave the bar with a woman and wound up with two, so much the better.

"Romeo?" Brittany said.

"Yeah?"

"That was a hell of a fight. Are you a boxer?"

"No and I didn't start the fight."

"You just finish them, hmm?"

"Yeah, you might say that endings are my business."

"No talking about work," Amber said. "Tonight we party."

"Fine by me," Tanner said.

He left the young ladies' apartment the following day, fully sated and with a request to return soon, but his mind had already begun to make plans about the best way to move forward.

It was time to get back to work.

2
VICE VERSA

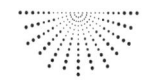

The Cabaret Strip Club in New York City was playing host to the heroes of the hour, as Merle and Earl Carter were finally being rewarded for their perceived killing of Tanner.

The club had been shut down for a week, as the FBI investigated the murders of Lars Gruber and Tanner, which they believed took place in the alleyway behind the club.

Gruber was indeed murdered, and by Tanner, while the other body carted off that night belonged to a mobster by the name of Jackie Verona, who Gruber himself had killed just hours before his death.

The conclusion the FBI came up with was that murders took place, but that they had no way of proving so, despite there being a photograph that showed the bodies. Still, the photo couldn't be positively linked to the location of the club, so the investigation was stalled, and the strip club reopened.

The Carter brothers had already been given the hundred grand in cash they had won as a reward for their presumed killing of Tanner, and on this night they were being led by hand back to the VIP rooms, each in the company of a young woman who would see to their pleasure.

They were not alone, as their generous host, Johnny Rossetti, had also decided to reward the men who had guarded the front doors, along with the other men who had guarded the alley. They were all present, except for Romeo, who had yet to return the calls made to his phone.

From where he was standing at the bar, Johnny Rossetti watched Merle and Earl as they entered their VIP rooms on the arms of hookers, then he turned to look at Carl the bartender.

"Hey, weren't you working the alley last week?"

"Yeah, but I don't need any reward, living through it was reward enough."

Johnny grinned. "I still can't believe you fainted, but fair's fair and I'll hook you up."

One of the dancers was on break inside a roped-off section at the side of the bar, and was wearing a white silk robe. She was a woman named Skye, who had large natural breasts and long dark hair. Johnny pointed at her as he talked to one of the barmaids.

"Go tell Skye I want to see her."

"Skye?" Carl said.

"You like her, right? I see you two talking all the time."

"Yeah, she's nice."

"You're gonna find out just how nice when she gives you a lap dance, but don't expect anything more from her, she's not a hooker. I only got pros for the Carter brothers. They deserve it for killing Tanner."

Skye appeared with a questioning look in her green eyes. "You wanted to see me, Johnny?"

"Yeah honey, Carl here is one of the heroes from last week. Take him back to VIP room six and show him a good time."

Skye smiled at Carl. "Follow me, sir."

Carl smiled back weakly and followed Skye toward the VIP rooms.

Johnny headed for his office but stopped as he saw Al Trent enter.

Trent was unshaven, and thick dark stubble covered his face, while his eyes looked red and swollen from lack of sleep and the jeans and green polo shirt he wore looked wrinkled.

"This is the first time I've seen you without a suit on Trent. But don't worry, I hear the state pen is giving away free suits. Nice orange jumpsuits."

Trent rushed toward Johnny and stuck a finger in his face.

"You framed me, didn't you?"

Two of the club's bouncers rushed over and Trent took a step backwards. One of the bouncers had a shaved head, while the other had a wide red scar on his left cheek, and both men were twice Trent's size, dressed all in black, and armed.

Johnny spoke to the man with the scar. "Pat him down, Bull."

The search took only a few seconds, and when it was done, the man spoke to Johnny as he held up the contents of Trent's pockets.

"He's clean, boss. No weapons, no bugs, but he does have a wallet, watch, and phone."

"Give them back to him when he leaves. Trent, follow me to my office."

Trent stared at his belongings for a moment, then he rushed to catch up to Johnny, who had already walked away.

"Just tell me why you framed me, Rossetti."

Johnny reached his office and held the door open for him.

"Get in here. I didn't frame you, but I can guess who did."

∼

Across the club in VIP room six, Carl swallowed hard as Skye removed the silk robe to reveal a red string bikini, and when she began gyrating her hips to music, he spoke. "Don't do that."

Skye cocked her head. "What?"

"You don't have to do that."

"Johnny wants you to have fun, and it's my job. Besides, it's not like you haven't seen me dance before."

"I know, Skye, but… that was different."

"How?"

"That was for other guys, people off the street, and I thought we were friends, sort of."

"We are friends; I mean we talk all the time. You've even met my daughter."

"How is Ashley?"

"She's good. She started high school this year."

"Get out of here. The last time I ran into you two at the supermarket she was just a little thing."

"Yeah, but she's grown like a weed the last few months."

"Really?"

"Um-hmm."

"See what I mean? If you do this, rub against me and whatever else, that's going to make things weird between us and we won't be friends anymore."

Skye stared at him for long moments without saying anything, then she put her robe back on and cut off the music.

"You really don't want me to give you a lap dance?"

"No."

"I could get one of the other girls if you'd like? I mean, I know I'm like the old lady here at thirty-two, and there's that new girl, the small blonde. I hear she's only nineteen."

"No, it's not that, you're not old and you're the most beautiful woman I've ever seen."

"What?"

Carl shrugged. "It's true."

Skye sat down beside Carl and took his hand.

"Didn't you say earlier that you were off this Sunday?"

"Yeah."

"So am I, and I want you to come to my apartment for dinner."

"What did you say?"

"Dinner, and I'm a good cook too."

"You want me to come to your apartment?"

"Yes, will you come?"

"Sure."

Skye kissed Carl on the lips. "You're a good man, Carl."

Carl blushed a bright red that made Skye laugh.

"I think you would have fainted if I had danced for you."

Carl sighed. "It wouldn't be the first time."

∼

"Why would Frank Richards want to frame me for murder?"

Johnny sent Trent a shrug, from where he sat on the sofa in his office.

"Maybe it's because you know too much."

Trent thought that over and realized it might be true. After all, he had gotten rid of Richards' wife for him and there were many other secrets he knew, or suspected, such as the true reason behind the upcoming meeting of The Conglomerate's elite, but that was something that even Richards wasn't aware he knew.

"Let's say you're right and it was Richards, why not just kill me instead?"

"I don't know, kid, and to tell you the truth, I really don't care. As far as I'm concerned, it couldn't happen to a nicer guy."

"You really didn't frame me?"

"No, but whoever it was did a great job of it. Not only do the cops want you for killing that guy, Reese, but the papers say they also have you linked to a murder that took place in some box factory."

"I don't know anything about either murder."

"Are you sure about that? Jackie Verona has gone missing and I seem to recall you telling me not to send him a warning." Johnny stood and walked over to study Trent carefully. "Did you kill Verona, kid?"

Trent turned and headed for the door. "I don't know whose blood and brain tissue they found in that warehouse and I didn't kill anybody."

Trent opened the door, but before he left, he gave Johnny a bit of news.

"Richards got the board to agree to demote you. You'll be summoned by him any day now."

"The son of a bitch wants to see me tomorrow, but he wouldn't tell me who was taking over. Do you know?"

"I don't; I only know you're out, and that's the one bright spot in my world right now."

Johnny waved a hand at Trent. "Go on, before I put you out of your misery."

"Somebody framed me, Rossetti, and when I find out who it was, I'll be back at Mr. Richards side."

"Sure kid, keep telling yourself that."

～

Johnny walked out into the club with Trent and watched him leave, then saw Merle and Earl walking toward him with wide eyes and silly grins.

They were dressed in new suits instead of their usual casual, and ratty, attire. The suits were a gift from Johnny, as were the women who had just pleasured them. Nothing was too good for the men who had killed Tanner.

Johnny smiled at them. "I see the girls showed you boys a good time. They should have, they cost three bills each."

Merle and Earl nodded at Johnny, and when they looked at each other, they giggled.

However, the biggest smile in the club belonged to Carl, who walked back to the bar with Skye on his arm. When they parted, Skye gave him a quick peck on the lips.

Johnny pointed at him as he went back behind the bar.

"Look at that grin; I guess Skye treated you right, hmm?"

"Vice versa," Skye said, and she sent Carl a wink as she returned to the stage.

3
LOOSE ENDS

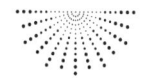

The following morning, at the rear of the MegaZenith building in Manhattan, Johnny stepped out of his limo as his driver, Mario, held the door open for him.

After taking a few steps toward the loading dock, Johnny stopped walking and placed a hand on Mario's shoulder.

"Get back in the limo; I'm going up alone."

Mario blinked in surprise, as his fat face scrunched up in concern. "Alone? But what if something happens?"

"If they want to whack me, they'll whack me, but there's no sense in both of us getting hit, but don't worry, I think this is the last place Richards would pick to kill me. Wait thirty minutes and if you don't hear from me, then get the hell out of here."

"I don't like it," Mario said.

"Me either, buddy, but one way or another I'm no longer the Underboss of the Family after today."

"Shit, so who's the new boss?"

"That's what I'm about to find out."

"You're sure you don't want me as backup, just in case?"

Johnny sent him a wink. "Stay here and I'll return with news in a few minutes."

Johnny walked up a set of concrete steps and disappeared into the shadows of the loading dock.

Mario let out a sigh and went back to the limo, where he leaned against it and smoked a cigar, as he checked his phone for messages.

When he saw that there was one from his daughter, he listened to it and felt distress as he heard her teary message.

"Daddy, it's Maria, please call me as soon as you can. I… I screwed up."

Mario phoned his daughter and heard the call being answered, but no one spoke.

"Hello? Maria, it's Daddy, baby, are you there?"

A female voice answered, but it was not his daughter's voice.

"Mr. Petrocelli, this is Special Agent Michelle Geary of the FBI, are you alone?"

"The FBI? What's going on? Where's my daughter?"

"We need to talk. I'll be at the Starbucks on East 57th Street at six o'clock. Refuse to meet with me and your daughter does time for dealing drugs."

"What? My girl's no dealer, she's a college kid."

"Apparently, the apple didn't fall far from the tree, Mario. Selling drugs is how you got your start, isn't it? We have her on video dealing drugs and if you don't play ball, she's going away for a long time."

"Let me speak to her."

"She'll be with me tonight, and if you don't join us by six, she'll be in a cell by seven. Remember, East 57th. Goodbye Mario."

The phone went dead and Mario let out a curse. After climbing back into the limo, he slumped in his seat, while wondering just how much the FBI had on his daughter and knowing that he would do anything they asked to see her clear of trouble.

Upstairs, on the sixtieth floor, Johnny was being greeted at the freight elevator by Richards' new assistant, a man named Robert Vance.

Vance was early thirties, tall, good-looking, and blond. His light-blue eyes scrutinized Johnny before he offered a hand in greeting.

"Mr. Rossetti, I don't know if you remember me, sir, but we met once while you were out in Las Vegas last year. My name is Robert Vance."

Johnny shook his hand. "I do remember you, and my late Uncle Al told me that you were the one who brokered peace between him and Richards."

"Yes, although by that time, Mr. Richards had already contracted with Tanner to have your uncle killed. Had I known that, I wouldn't have wasted my time making peace."

"Why not?"

"A contract is a contract, and despite your loss, I believe that Tanner acted in good faith."

"Even after Richards told him to stand down?"

"As I said, a contract is a contract, but please follow me to Mr. Richards' office, he's waiting for you."

"They frisked me downstairs. That's the first time that's happened."

"Just a precaution, and your weapon will be returned. Also, Mr. Richards will have a bodyguard present."

They walked together in silence. When they reached the office, Vance motioned for Johnny to enter alone.

"You know, Al Trent used to sit in on meetings."

"Yes, sir and perhaps someday I'll gain that level of trust as well, but for now, I'm off to run an errand."

Johnny stared at Vance for several seconds, then offered his hand. "Come by the Cabaret Strip Club sometime and we'll talk."

"I might do that," Vance said, as he ended the handshake and opened the door for Johnny to enter.

Johnny walked in and took a seat in front of the desk. Standing by the window behind the desk was the promised bodyguard, a middle-aged man named Gary. Gary was large, but by no means huge, and his gray eyes kept a close watch on Johnny.

Richards made a show of releasing a great sigh as he shook his head sadly.

"If you had only handled Tanner in a timely fashion I wouldn't be forced to demote you, however, as things stand, the board feels that it's time for fresh blood at the helm."

Johnny looked over at Gary and saw the bulge of a shoulder holster beneath the suit jacket he was wearing.

"Fresh blood at the helm, or spilled here in the office?"

"You won't be harmed, just demoted."

"Sam Giacconi is on the board and as his proxy I should have been allowed to vote."

"Your vote would have resulted in a tie and no action would have been taken against you, but you're an Underboss, not a Don, so we didn't bother to count it."

"That's bullshit and you know it. Ever since Sam went into the nursing home I've been acting in his place."

"In any event, the deed is done, and you've been removed as leader."

"All right then, who is my replacement?"

"I've chosen Joe Pullo. He's a man who has proven himself loyal time and again and I'm sure he'll continue to do so as Underboss of The Giacconi Crime Family."

"Joe?"

"You disagree with the choice?"

"I disagree with the decision, but… Pullo's a good man, and smart too."

"You are to act as his adviser, his Consigliere, as you people like to call it. Will you do it?"

Johnny sneered. "I want to keep living, so yes, I'll do it."

Richards grinned. "Excellent, and as the new boss, Pullo will be taking your place at the meeting Sunday as well. That's all, and from now on, my new man, Vance, will make contact if I need to speak to Mr. Pullo. Oh, and by the way, the Cabaret Strip Club now belongs to Pullo; let's call it a perk of leadership."

Johnny stood up in a rush and Gary brought his gun out. "That club is mine! I built it from the ground up."

Richards grinned again. "You'll sign it over by the day of the board meeting or blood will be spilled, your choice."

Johnny balled his hands into fists as he struggled to keep calm; when he could speak again, he asked a question.

"Anything else?"

The grin had left Richards' face, only to be replaced by a smug look of satisfaction.

"We're done, but I want to say one more thing. You've only yourself to blame for this. Your ineptitude at handling the Tanner situation was epic, including the loss of Lars Gruber."

"Tanner was the best. It's as simple as that, but in the end, my men handled him."

"Tanner was a bug, and let me remind you that you no longer have men. From now on you'll simply follow orders from Pullo."

"Yeah and those orders come from you."

Richards dismissed him with a wave. "As I said before, we're done."

Johnny headed for the door, eager to leave.

∼

JOHNNY LEFT THE OFFICE WITHOUT ANOTHER WORD AND STRODE off toward the freight elevator, as Richards watched him leave.

"Gary."

"Yes, sir?"

"Make certain that Mr. Rossetti has left the premises. Afterwards, go find Al Trent and bring him back here."

"Yes, sir," Gary said, and left the office.

Richards rose from his seat and gazed out at the city, which was spread before him.

This is a good day to tie up loose ends, and once the meeting of the board is over, I'll be the only one left standing.

Richards poured himself a drink and smiled as he thought about what was to come.

4

NEVER INSULT A MAN'S RIDE

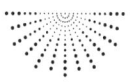

Tanner returned to the farm and found Tim rushing toward him while holding a newspaper. They were standing on the farmhouse's wide front porch. The house sat in a clearing surrounded by trees, with the barn behind it and a graveled driveway leading in from the road.

"Tanner, I think I know how to access Richards' files."

"You've cracked the encryption?"

"No, but look here. Al Trent was indicted on two counts of murder. I'll bet you anything he could get into those files."

"Yes, but we discussed this and agreed that he wouldn't give that info up even under threat of death."

"That's true, he wouldn't give it up to you, because he would believe that you'd kill him anyway, but he would give it up to me."

"And why would he do that? Are you planning to torture him?"

"Of course not, but I don't have to. I can give him something he wants, something he desperately needs; a new identity, one that he can use to escape the law."

Tanner stared at Tim. "How's Madison feel about that plan?"

Tim's enthusiasm deflated. "I... haven't mentioned it to her."

"I framed Trent for her, so that Trent would pay for killing her mother. I think this plan should be her call."

"Yeah, you're right."

"There's another thing, even if she agrees, there's no guarantee that Al Trent will take the deal. Plus, once he knows he's dealing with you, he might try to trade you to The Conglomerate and use their help to disappear."

"I hadn't thought of that, but it's worth the risk and you'll be there to back me up, or rather, Romeo will."

"Speaking of Romeo, I'll be heading back to New York tonight. I need to get an inside view of what's been going on."

"That's risky, isn't it?"

Tanner gave a slight shrug. "No risk, no reward."

Tim smiled at him. "I noticed you didn't come back last night. I guess you made friends with one of the locals."

"You could say that, but it's too risky to stay in this area long term, so start thinking about where you want to relocate to when all this is over."

Tim waved an arm around. "We have been thinking of relocating, but it's as safe as can be here. There's no way anybody can track us down."

"I've killed more than a few men who had that very same thought when they tried to hide from me. Anybody can be found, Tim. It just depends on how badly the person looking wants to find you."

~

AT THAT VERY MOMENT IN SOUTHERN NEW JERSEY, AL TRENT was speaking with a man named Eric, who ran the personnel office for Tri-State Janitorial Services.

Tri-State Janitorial Services employed the late Carl Reese,

one of two men that Trent had been indicted of killing. Tri-State was also the company whose computers Tim hacked into, to infiltrate MegaZenith.

Trent came to Tri-State looking for the answer to who framed him. He believed the trip would likely be a waste of time, but when Eric whispered to him that he would like to speak to Trent in private, Trent knew that he had been right to come there.

Trent left Tri-State, and now he and Eric were meeting for lunch at a diner on Route 70, one that was two towns away from Tri-State's headquarters.

Trent had arrived first and ordered coffee for both of them. He hadn't touched his and he spoke to Eric as soon as the man slid across from him in the booth. Trent also took note of the envelope Eric was carrying.

"What is it you know?"

Eric was in his mid-thirties with brown hair and brown eyes. His height was average, but he had the beginnings of a gut.

"I know that I want to be paid for the information I have."

"All I've got on me is three hundred and change."

"What about that watch you're wearing? It looks expensive."

"It's an Omega and worth more than that car you drove up in."

Eric laughed. "You're a snotty bastard, aren't you? Give me the watch and I'll tell you what I know; otherwise, I walk away and deny we ever met."

Trent's gaze flicked to the envelope.

"What's in there?"

"Something that might help you. You see, I don't think you killed Carl, but inside this envelope are pictures of the people who I think did kill him."

"I don't understand."

A waitress appeared and asked if they wanted anything else. When they both declined, she walked away, and Eric continued.

"Carl came here for training and it was a day or two before he was killed. That's when we discovered that a couple of corporate spies had infiltrated our company to gain access to MegaZenith. Carl told me he was going to blackmail them and now he's dead."

"Why didn't you tell the police about this?"

"And confess to being part of a blackmail plot? No thanks, plus, I'd probably get fired, and it might put me on the killer's radar, so when I give this to you, use it however you want, but keep me out of it."

"Are there names to go with those pictures?"

"Yeah, but they're fakes and when I checked again, after I heard that Carl got killed, all of their info was gone from our system. The only reason I have these photos is because I printed them out the day Carl was here, actually, right after he left."

Trent played with his watchband.

"I'll give you all the money I have in my wallet and five thousand more. I can transfer it to you today."

Eric shook his head. "Uh-uh, I like that watch and besides, you insulted my car."

Trent ripped the watch from his wrist and slid it across the table, then he yanked the envelope from Eric's hand and opened it.

Inside were two photos, showing a man and a woman each.

Trent recognized both of them. They were the photos that Tim had used to set-up his and Madison's fake IDs at MegaZenith.

Madison's involvement both perplexed and angered Trent, while learning that she was involved with the hacker, Tim Jackson, left him mystified.

"What did Reese say about these two?"

"Carl said that they were a couple. He had a thing for the girl. My guess is that he tried to pressure them too much and they killed him, but why frame you? Do you know them?"

Trent said nothing more; he just rose from the booth and walked out to his car. He had to get back to the city and find Madison, and once he did, he'd have answers. He also planned to make her pay for using him. And as far as Tim Jackson was concerned, Trent considered him a dead man.

5
HE'S BACK

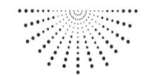

Sara checked her appearance one more time before leaving her apartment and hailing a taxi.

The last week of her life had been one of the strangest to her.

She had always been a woman driven by passion, by goals, and some would say, by obsession.

For years, her obsession was The Bureau, and her goal was to be its first female Director. That desire became meaningless to her when the man she loved was killed. From that day forward, only revenge fueled her.

With Tanner believed to be dead, she had been feeling like a rudderless ship, that is, until she found a new target for her wrath.

While it was true that Tanner had killed her lover, he did so on orders, and by his own admission, those orders came from Frank Richards, the CEO of MegaZenith, who covertly was a ruling member of a criminal organization named The Conglomerate.

So now, she had a new target with new goals fueled by the same sense of revenge.

She would use anything and anyone to get to Richards, but

all her bridges to the FBI had been burned when she left. All but one that is.

Her former partner, Jake Garner, was attracted to her. Through him, she could gain information that might aid her and, if she were truthful about it, she was attracted to Garner as well.

She knew from their past association that Garner often stopped for drinks after work at a restaurant in Midtown. Sara decided that it would be good to run into him again.

Her plan was to have a late lunch at the restaurant and linger over drinks until Garner finally showed.

She was dressed casually, but still with an eye toward seduction and had no qualms about using Garner to get information. The man had broken a hundred hearts if he'd broken one and might not even be capable of having a serious relationship. He wouldn't lose his heart to her and she believed that she no longer had one to give. No, her heart died along with her lover, Brian Ames.

~

THE RESTAURANT WAS NAMED MARTINO'S AND IT SERVED ITALIAN cuisine.

Sara spotted Garner as he was leaving and was surprised that he had been drinking so early in the afternoon. She was about to call out to him when she noticed his companion.

The woman was blonde, beautiful, and looking at Garner with great interest as he spoke.

Garner must have said something humorous, because the woman let out a laugh and touched him on the arm. Seconds later, the two of them climbed into a taxi and sped off, and if Sara had to guess, they were headed to bed.

It didn't surprise her to find Garner with a woman, but she was still filled with anger and felt betrayed.

The blonde had been her sister, Jennifer. Sara had warned

Garner away from her because she knew that he would break Jenny's heart with his love 'em and leave 'em approach.

Sara was pissed, and the anger came not only from the fact that she believed her sister was headed for heartache, but also from another emotion, jealousy.

Although she wouldn't admit it to herself, she wanted Jake Garner, and not just as a source of information. She was jealous that her sister was sleeping with him and it was a feeling she didn't like one bit.

∼

JOHNNY ARRIVED AT THE CLUB AND WAS SO LOST IN THOUGHT that he hadn't noticed the redhead rushing toward him as he stepped from the limo.

"I need to speak with you, Johnny."

Johnny looked up with a start, but then smiled. "Hello Sophia, any news about your father?"

Sophia Verona pushed past Mario and got up in Johnny's face. She was the daughter of Jackie Verona, and a member of The Calvino Crime Family.

"The word is that The Conglomerate had my father hit. What would you know about that?"

"I don't know a thing, honey, really. But if I had to guess, I'd say he was killed by Lars Gruber."

"Gruber is dead."

"Yeah, but Jackie went missing the day Gruber arrived here."

Sophia looked thoughtful. She was a beautiful woman in her early thirties who ran a squad of cyber thieves. She was the top earner for the Calvino Family, but because she was a woman, she wouldn't even be considered to take her father's place as Underboss, but in truth, she was well liked by the troops and tough enough to lead them.

"Sophia?"

"Hmm?"

"What's Vic Conti say about all this? He runs the Calvino's. Does he think Jackie is dead?"

"No one really knows what to think, but Saul Adamo keeps pushing to take his place."

"Adamo? He's not smart enough to step into Jackie's shoes."

"Frank Richards had the board appoint him, and yeah, you're not the only one not happy about it. I think it means he had something to do with my father's disappearance."

"Saul and your father do hate each other, so how is he treating you?"

"Not good, he sent one of his men over to learn our system. I think he's getting ready to push me out… or worse. I also think he wants to push Vic out and take over."

Johnny placed a hand under her chin. "If there's any trouble, come here, and I'll make sure you're safe."

"I can handle myself, you know?"

"Believe me I know it, but I want you to know that you can come to me."

Sophia smiled. "Why? For old time sake?"

"Yeah, it's been years since we broke up, but I still care about you."

"I know that and it's why I came here. I knew you wouldn't bullshit me, and if Gruber did kill my father, then it was Frank Richards that ordered the hit."

Johnny gripped her arm. "Don't do anything stupid like going after Richards; you wouldn't live through it."

Sophia wrenched her arm free as anger lit her green eyes. "I'm more worried about Richards coming after me," she said, then marched back toward her car.

⁓

Johnny entered his office and found Joe Pullo sitting before the desk.

MAKING A KILLING ON WALL STREET

"I've been told that your rightful place is behind that desk now, Joe, or would you rather I started calling you Mr. Pullo?"

Pullo stood. He was wearing a black suit with the jacket hanging open and the holster on his left hip was visible, as was the gun it held, while his right arm was in a white sling because of his shoulder injury.

Pullo's brown hair, which had receded, was cut short, but his eyebrows were bushy and compensated for the hairline, while the eyes beneath them broadcast his intelligence.

Johnny was standing in the center of the office and Pullo walked over and stood before him.

"My grandfather worked with Sam Giacconi when they were both just a couple of button men for the old Tarsi Family, did you know that?"

Johnny nodded. "Yeah, I heard Sam mention it."

"My father did collections, broke the bones of the late payers, and whacked the ones who needed it. He did that right up until the time he was killed by the Calvino Family, back before we made peace with them. Old Albertino Calvino himself shot my father to death when I was just eight years old, did you also know that?"

"Yes, I did," Johnny said, and he also heard that it was Joe Pullo who made the crime boss disappear and that Pullo had only been fifteen at the time.

"The day after my father died, Sam Giacconi comes to the house and tells my mother that she didn't have to worry about anything. He had been shot too, a leg wound, but he took the time in the middle of a war to come and comfort my mother. I never forgot that."

Johnny said nothing, but he nodded again. That was the Sam Giacconi he knew, a real leader and a class act.

"The next day, I showed up at that candy store he used to own and told him I wanted to work. He paid me to sweep the floors and stock shelves. By the time I was ten, I was running numbers and I made my bones just a few years later."

"I get it, Joe. You're saying that you've earned the right to lead the Family."

A slight smile curved Pullo's lips, as he shook his head.

"No, Johnny, you don't get it. When Sam started getting sick with the Alzheimer's he told me that he was putting you in charge. He said that I was to think of you as if you were him, and that if anyone threatened you, that I was to take them out."

"What are you saying?"

Pullo got down on one knee and bowed his head. "I don't care what Richards or anyone else wants. I work for Sam Giacconi, which means I work for you. You are my Don, my loyalty and my life, they're yours."

Johnny gazed down at Pullo with awe showing on his face. He reached down and gripped Pullo beneath his good arm.

"Stand up."

Pullo rose and the two men stood silently before each other, until Johnny embraced him with a hug.

"You're an even better man than I knew."

When Johnny released him, Pullo asked a question.

"So, what's our next move?"

Johnny smiled. "You and I are going for a ride. There's something I need to show you."

"I take it by that smile that it's good news?"

"The best, buddy, but listen, for now, we need to make Richards think that he's in control, so when we're not alone, you're the boss and I'm just your adviser."

"I get it, but this Conglomerate thing has gotten out of hand when they're the ones picking who runs the family."

"That's what we're going to talk about when we get where we're going."

"Talk about it with who?"

"You'll see when we get there, but just know this, things are about to change."

"Are we going to war?"

"Maybe, but there's a chance we won't have to, but c'mon, we'll take your Hummer."

"No limo? So even Mario doesn't know where you're taking me?"

"No and you're the only one I would trust with this."

Joe stopped Johnny as he put his hand on the doorknob to leave. "What's going on?"

Johnny took Pullo's face between his hands and grinned.

"He's back, Joe, the old man is back."

"What? Sam? How?"

"An experimental drug treatment for Alzheimer's disease, and damn if it didn't work. Sam is back."

Pullo's grin matched Johnny's as he opened the door. "Take me to him," Pullo said and both men rushed from the club.

6
YOU CAN'T TRUST A WEASEL

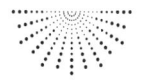

Merle and Earl Carter stood together inside their hotel room and gazed in at the contents of their room safe.

They were looking at the hundred grand in cash that The Conglomerate had paid them as a reward for killing Tanner. There was just one problem; Tanner wasn't dead.

"We can't spend it," Merle said.

"I know," Earl agreed.

They had moved out of the hooker-infested motel they had been staying in and now shared a room in a downtown hotel that catered to the tourist trade.

The money to do so came from Sara, who had paid the boys a handsome sum for not only killing Tanner, but also as a reward for earlier having saved her from being raped and possibly killed.

Sara's money they spent freely, because although she would be furious with them for tricking her if Tanner showed up, they didn't fear that she would kill them. Well, they didn't fear it very much. The Conglomerate would kill them, so they didn't dare spend a penny of the reward money.

"Think of all the things we could buy with that," Merle said.

"I am, and it makes me sick that we can't touch it," Earl said.

"Maybe Tanner will stay dead."

"Maybe, but what if he don't? He could show up years from now and we'd still be screwed."

"Earl."

"Yeah?"

"I hate Tanner."

"Me too."

~

AT THE FARMHOUSE IN PENNSYLVANIA, TANNER HALTED HIS RUN as he spotted Tim and Madison out for a walk.

As the three of them traveled along together, Tim explained to Madison the deal he wanted to make with Al Trent.

Madison had listened without commenting, but when Tim finished, she looked over at Tanner.

"What do you think about this?"

"As I told Tim, it's your decision, but I'd rather not do it."

"Why?"

"Trent sounds like a weasel, and you can't trust a weasel."

They walked on in silence, loosely following a stream that ran through the property.

When they came to the spot where the stream flowed downward from a steep incline, they crested the small hill, walked through a narrow band of trees, and stepped into a clearing, where a building stood, and which had only been half completed.

The structure was three stories high with a steel frame. The concrete floors were laid in, along with the walls and roof, but it had no doors or windows. Pipes were visible that would have been the plumbing system, but the aborted building had never been connected to the well water on the property.

The structure was one reason that the land had been

inexpensive. In 2008, the farm had been sold to a developer who had inside information that the surrounding area would be part of a new East-West highway that would stretch from Southern New Jersey to Ohio.

The developer reasoned that the value of the land would skyrocket and managed to get a vast portion of the farmland rezoned for commercial use.

If all had gone as expected, millions would have been made, but as is often the case, things changed for the worse.

The economy tanked as they broke ground for what was to be the first of four office buildings; unfortunate, but easily handled by delaying completion of the other buildings. However, when the word came out of Washington, DC, that the highway project had been cancelled, the developer found himself the owner of a half-completed office building, even as his existing buildings lost tenants at an alarming rate, due to the downturn in the economy.

The project was abandoned, the property put up for sale, and after spending years as an eyesore on the developer's balance sheet, it was sold to Tim for pennies on the dollar.

In the years the farm sat abandoned, the locals gave the place a name. They called it Forgotten Farm.

The office building saw use at night as a make-out spot for local teens, who used its third floor as a sort of lookout point, to view the nearby stream and dormant fields.

Tanner investigated the building when they first arrived and discovered food wrappers, used condoms, and remnants of marijuana cigarettes, along with a stack of beer cans in one corner that was three feet high.

It also appeared as if the teens were using the different sized, empty wooden wire reels left behind as tables and chairs.

The kids never came near the farmhouse, so Tanner left them alone to have their fun, and Tim and Madison agreed with the decision.

Madison reached down and picked up a piece of rusted

rebar, one of the many pieces of scrap left behind when the project ended.

"I don't want to do it. I want Al to go to prison. It's what he deserves for murdering my mom."

Tim sighed. "Then that's it, we won't do it. And I guess we'll go back to Tanner's plan, infiltrating the upcoming meeting of The Conglomerate's big shots, but Tanner, how are you going to do it?"

"I'm not sure yet, which is why 'Romeo' needs to go back and gather more info."

Madison stared at him with a concerned expression. "Everyone thinks you're dead, why not just walk away and let things be?"

"I can't. There are loose ends that need tying up, and this was never about running; this was about winning. The men who control The Conglomerate think that they can either own me or kill me, but I'm going to make them see that they can't do either one, and that I'm nobody's puppet."

Madison kissed Tanner on the cheek. "Please be careful."

A sound came from their right and Tim pointed at a group of trees.

"Your friend is back, Madison."

It was a dog, a female, with some German shepherd in her. She was so skinny her ribs showed. Madison had been leaving food for the dog recently, by the rear porch steps at night, and had watched her eat from the window. The dog would follow them, but she never came near, and Tanner suspected that she had made a home inside the incomplete structure.

Madison called to the dog. The hound moved closer, then sat.

"She still doesn't trust me."

"It's a hard thing to earn," Tanner said.

They began the trek back toward the farmhouse and Tanner asked them about their plans.

"What about you two? Where do you go from here?"

"We're thinking of heading south," Tim said. "Madison and I like the farm and we'll either keep it as a safe house or put it up for sale, but it's too rural for my tastes in the long run, and we'll probably head to Atlanta, or maybe Miami."

"One way or another, things will change at this meeting on Sunday," Tanner said. "And your theft of Conglomerate funds will be at the bottom of their things to worry about. With your new IDs, you should be safe."

Madison looked past Tim to speak to Tanner. "If you're going to play Romeo, we'll have to dye your hair again and apply the tattoos."

Tanner nodded. "Romeo needs to head back to Manhattan."

"And back into the lion's den?" Tim said.

Tanner smiled. "I'll feel right at home there."

7
THE GHOST AND THE WICKED WITCH

"What are you gawking at, Joey? You look like you've seen a ghost."

Those words were spoken by eighty-six-year-old Sam Giacconi. Giacconi had never been a large man and age had shrunken him. He was lined with wrinkles and his flesh was mottled by age, but his eyes held a fierceness that could rival the fire in Tanner's gaze.

Johnny had given Joe directions to a long-term care facility, and as they drove, he filled him in on Sam Giacconi's condition.

Giacconi had been part of an experimental treatment to cure Alzheimer's, and of the fifty-six patients receiving the treatment, Giacconi was one of the forty-seven patients who responded to the protocol, which included drugs, memory drills, and physical exercise. Giacconi's memory wasn't perfect, but it was better than many his age, and the researchers were hopeful that it was a permanent cure.

Sam Giacconi was in a wheelchair. He had a bad hip before succumbing to Alzheimer's and the subsequent inactivity only aggravated the condition.

Pullo grabbed Giacconi's offered hand, then leaned down

and embraced him gently about the shoulders. When he released the old man, he shook his head in wonder.

"It's a miracle."

"You're telling me. Until two weeks ago, I was lost in the past, locked away inside my own head. Hell, Joey, when the docs asked what year it was, I said it was 2012, because that was the last year I remembered."

Pullo shook his head again. "It's a goddamn miracle. The last time I visited you, you thought I was my grandfather."

Giacconi looked over at Johnny. "Does he know?"

"Yeah, Sam, Richards told Joe that he's in charge, and when I told Joe, he pledged to keep following me, because it's what you wanted. That's why I brought him here."

Giacconi looked at Pullo with pride shining in his eyes.

"I knew you were a stand-up guy, Joey, but to just give up your power that way, that's above and beyond."

"I take orders from you, Sam. The last thing you said to me was to protect Johnny and to treat him as if he were you, and that's all I did. What I want to know is, what are we going to do about this Conglomerate thing? It's getting out of hand."

Giacconi rolled his wheelchair over to a table, which was in the kitchen area of his spacious private room.

"You two sit and I'll tell you what we're gonna do."

"You've got a plan?" Johnny asked.

"I've got a plan," Giacconi said. "And it's gonna put us back in charge like we should be."

~

MARIO ARRIVED AT STARBUCKS EARLY AND FOUND HIS DAUGHTER sitting with a man and a woman, and the two of them had Fed written all over them.

It was Jake Garner, along with his new partner, Special Agent Michelle Geary, a woman in her early forties with blonde hair and a shapely figure.

Maria looked up at her father with wet eyes. "I'm so sorry, Daddy."

Mario sat beside her and took her hand. "It's okay, baby. I'll straighten this out."

"Mr. Petrocelli, I'm Special Agent Michelle Geary and this is my partner, Special Agent Jake Garner. We have evidence that your daughter was trafficking in drugs and we will arrest her for it… if necessary."

Mario was sweating even though his hands felt like ice. He was scared to death for his daughter, whose dream was to become a lawyer. Something that wouldn't happen if she were convicted of trafficking in drugs.

"What evidence do you have?"

Geary opened a laptop, hit a few buttons, and spun the machine around so that Mario could see the screen. It took a second for the video to load, but when it did, it showed his daughter in a setting that appeared to be a park.

A hidden camera and microphone followed Maria as she walked to a bench and handed the lone man sitting there a shopping bag. The man thanked her and passed her a white envelope. Within seconds after the exchange, several men and women in suits and uniforms were yelling at Maria to get on the ground. The video ended with a confused and terrified Maria being knocked off her feet and shoved face-first into the grass.

Maria grabbed her father's arm. She was a cute girl of nineteen with dark hair and dark eyes.

"I'm not selling drugs. A friend of mine from school, Kimberly, she handed me that bag and asked me to take it to her brother, the man on the bench. I didn't know there were drugs in the bag and I don't know where the marijuana came from either."

"What marijuana?"

Maria wiped tears away as she talked. "They found marijuana in my purse and they say there was cocaine in that bag. Daddy, I swear on Mama's memory that I'm innocent. Kimberly must have set me up."

"I believe you, baby," Mario said, as he stared across at the two FBI agents.

The woman had an evil little smirk on her face, while the man looked confused, and Mario briefly wondered if he hadn't been in on the set up. If not, it didn't matter. Cops were all the same, and he'd back up his partner's play even if he didn't agree with her tactics.

Mario wasn't the brightest man, but he knew a frame when he saw one and he also knew his daughter. Maria was innocent.

After taking a deep breath to calm himself, he spoke to the woman.

"My daughter leaves here now, never sees you again, and we have a deal."

"You understand what we're asking?"

"Yeah, and we have a deal, but my daughter goes free."

Geary smiled. "Evidence goes missing all the time."

"No evidence, no trial, not even an arrest. She leaves here and goes back to her life."

"Agreed, but you'll have to deliver."

Maria was looking back and forth at them. "What's going on?"

Mario smiled at her. "Everything's good, you just go home and I'll be there later."

"What do they want you to do?"

"We're just going to talk. Now leave and I'll see you later."

"Daddy?"

Mario kissed her on the forehead. "Go baby, and don't worry about a thing."

Maria rose from the table hesitantly, and after another assurance by her father, she drifted out onto the street and disappeared among the crowd.

Mario glared at the two FBI agents. "You bastards play hardball; I'll give you that."

Geary leaned across the table. "I'll tell you what you're going to give us; you're going to give us Johnny Rossetti and the rest of your scumbag friends on a platter, because if you don't, I'll personally see to it that your daughter does hard time."

Mario swallowed a cold lump down his throat as he looked into Geary's eyes, and knew that he was in a world of shit.

8
ROMEO RETURNS

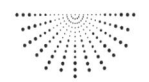

Tanner, in the guise of Romeo, returned to New York City and was standing on the corner of East 38th and looking across the street at Laurel Ivy's townhouse.

He knew that she must believe him to be dead, but he also knew that when he revealed to her that he was alive, that she would keep his secret for as long as he asked her to.

He was about to cross the street when he recognized a man coming from the other way, and he moved back beneath the shadows of the tree he had been standing under.

The man was Joe Pullo.

Pullo climbed the steps of Laurel's townhouse and rang the doorbell. When Laurel appeared in the doorway, Tanner felt his heart beat faster, and for the thousandth time he wondered what it was about her that affected him like no one else.

Laurel greeted Pullo with a bright smile and a kiss on the cheek.

When Tanner saw that Pullo only rated the cheek and not the lips, he smiled without knowing it. Still, it appeared that Pullo and Laurel were friends, and possibly dating, and that meant that more than kissing could soon follow.

Tanner turned away, perplexed to no end by the emotions

frothing inside him, and as he had done for years, he struggled to push Laurel Ivy from his mind.

∼

He arrived at the strip club a short time later, knowing that he need not be concerned about running into Pullo.

He had traveled by subway and walked to the club. When he neared the entrance, he saw four masked men rushing toward the door with their guns drawn.

One of the men shot the bouncer who was standing outside smoking, while another man caught sight of Tanner, who was dressed in Romeo's signature leather vest, bolo tie, and tight black jeans.

As the man took aim, Tanner whipped out his gun and shot the man twice in the chest. The man fell, and his three friends turned on Tanner, but Tanner was already firing on them and hit a second man in the leg, which caused the thug to fall to the ground and lose his weapon.

Of the two men left, one went down from a fatal shot to the neck delivered by the club's wounded bouncer. Upon seeing this, the last man grabbed up his friend with the wounded leg and dragged him back toward their car, where a driver waited behind the wheel, and the car sped off just as two more bouncers ran out of the club.

The wounded bouncer shouted to his partners. "Don't shoot the blond dude; he saved my ass."

Tanner approached the group slowly, with his gun held loose at his side, and one of the bouncers pointed at him.

"Yeah, that's Romeo; he was here last week when Tanner got wasted."

The wounded bouncer spoke again. "You saved me, dude, the fuckers were about to shoot me again."

Tanner answered as Romeo. "Man, I just came here to look

at some ass and have a drink, and that's when everything went all World War III and shit."

The wounded bouncer had been hit in the side. The wound was dripping blood, but didn't look to be serious, as the bullet had passed through one of the man's love handles.

When the senior bouncer told one of the other men to take the wounded man to see a doctor, Tanner figured they were probably talking about Laurel Ivy. He smiled as he realized it would interrupt her date with Pullo.

"Romeo?"

His name was called by the senior bouncer, a man named Bull who was nearly the size of his namesake and had a scar on his left cheek.

"Yeah, boss?" Tanner said.

"Hear those sirens? That means it's time for you to hide. Go inside and stay in the office, I'm sure Johnny will want to talk to you."

"Him and the cops both."

"No, we'll make a few calls and keep the club out of this. Now give me your gun and I'll hide it with the others."

After taking Tanner's gun, Bull reached down and pulled the masks off the dead men. When he pulled the mask off the man Tanner had killed, he straightened abruptly.

"Son of a bitch, that's Sammy Vega. He's a member of the Calvino Family."

Tanner stared down at the man. He thought he had stopped a robbery, but it appeared that he might have interrupted something more serious.

Bull handed him the masks and tossed his head toward the door. "Get inside and wait in the office."

Tanner did as he was told and found the club looking normal, as music blared, and men hooted at near-naked women.

Outside, the shots had seemed like thunder, but apparently,

they couldn't compete with the throb of the music and the raucous crowd.

Carl was behind the bar, but he paid no attention to Tanner because he was busy mixing drinks.

Tanner went inside the office, hid the bloody masks in the base of a fake plant that was sitting in a corner, and took a seat on the sofa to think.

He thought he had stopped a heist, but he had stopped an act of aggression by The Calvino Crime Family, a Family whose Underboss had been Jackie Verona.

With Verona gone, someone was looking to take over, and that someone was making a move on the Giacconi Family while they were still weakened from their war with him.

Tanner smirked. It was a smart move, start a war, which would be blamed on the Calvino's boss, Vic Conti, only Tanner had never heard Conti described as a warmonger.

With Jackie Verona missing and assumed dead, someone else in The Calvino Family was making a power grab, and only days before the upcoming council meeting, a bold move, and they wouldn't be very happy with Romeo when they learned he had interfered.

Tanner touched the R clasp hanging from the bolo tie.

"Romeo, I think you stumbled into a mess."

∼

Johnny returned to the club around midnight, after the police had left and the bodies had been toted away.

Tanner was sitting in the office with Bull, who had brought him his weapon, along with a beer and cheeseburger from the bar. When Johnny walked in, Bull stood and told him what had happened, including the fact that one of the dead men was from the Calvino Family.

Johnny shook his head. "Saul Adamo must be crazy if he thinks he can just roll in and take our territory away."

"I thought Conti ran the Calvinos?" Bull said.

"He does, but I've been told that Adamo is making moves now that Jackie has disappeared."

"Maybe he's crazy like a fox," Bull said. "We have lost a lot of men lately thanks to that bastard Tanner."

"I'll call Joe Pullo and bring him up to speed. I'll also call Vic Conti and see what he says about this."

"Adamo will think twice now before trying anything again," Bull said.

"How's Tony doing, Bull?"

"He just called, said he'll be fine, but Doc Ivy told him to rest for a couple of days."

Johnny smiled at Romeo. "You did us a solid, and thanks to you they never entered the club. Not only would they have robbed us, but they might have hurt a customer."

"I just came here for a drink and to look at some ass, but I'm ready for trouble when it comes, you know?"

"Where are you from?"

"LA, but I got family here, over in Jersey."

"Do you need me, boss?" Bull asked.

"No, you go back into the club, and that was good work tonight."

Bull nodded toward Romeo. "We had help, and if he wasn't so small, I'd put him on my crew."

"Yo, I ain't no elephant like you, but I'm big where it counts."

Bull laughed. "See ya around, Romeo."

When Bull left, Johnny grabbed the chair from behind the desk and rolled it around to the other side of the coffee table to sit across from Romeo, who was seated on the sofa.

"Do you always wear those mirrored sunglasses?"

"Yeah, it's like, part of my look, you know?"

Johnny reached into his pocket and brought out a roll of cash. After counting out a thousand dollars, he laid it in front of Romeo.

"I'm putting you on the payroll, a thousand a week to start. What do you say?"

Tanner scooped up the money and shoved it in a side pocket.

"I'll take this for what I did tonight, and if you need help, I'm here, but I stay my own man."

"It can be cold out there on your own, Romeo."

"Maybe man, but there ain't no team in I."

Johnny leaned back in his seat and thought for a moment, before straightening back up and speaking.

"I've got a special project for you."

∼

UPTOWN, JAKE GARNER SIGHED AS HE WATCHED MARIO LEAVE the building where the FBI headquarters was housed. He and his new partner, Michelle Geary, had ridden down in the elevator with Mario, after hours of interrogation.

"That fat fuck gave us very little this time," Geary said. "But by the time I'm through with him, he'll be a star witness at Johnny Rossetti's trial."

"You set up his daughter, didn't you?"

"Of course, the stupid girl was gullible, but we have her on video delivering drugs to a known dealer and that's all that matters."

Garner spoke through clenched teeth. "This isn't how I work, Michelle, and I don't think Marty will like it either."

"You're going to snitch to the boss about this, why? Mario Petrocelli will do whatever we want now and once we wire him up, we'll learn more in a week than we have in the last year."

"Maybe so, but this isn't right, and you know it. It's why you kept me in the dark."

"I get results, Jake, and you'll profit by them as much as I will, partner. The Johnny Rossettis of the world don't play by the rules, so why should we?"

"Because we're supposed to be better than they are."

"We are better, because we're going to win and take them off the streets."

Garner headed for the door. "I'm going home."

"Do that and think about what I said. When we put Rossetti away, our careers will advance, count on it."

Garner left the building and caught a cab. When he was halfway home, he checked his phone for messages and saw that Sara had left one asking to meet him for lunch at a midtown restaurant the next day.

He texted her back, agreeing to meet, then texted her sister, Jennifer.

He didn't know what Sara wanted to see him about, but it was time she knew that he and her sister had gotten together, and also why. He sent one more text and wondered what Sara's reaction would be once they all met.

"Not good," he mumbled to himself.

Sara, his ex-partner, had shot him, and now Geary, his new partner, was trying to lead him down a dangerous path of backdoor justice.

Garner sighed and thought that maybe he should have been a doctor like his mother wanted him to be.

9
WHAT YOU SEE IS WHAT YOU GET

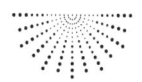

THE FOLLOWING MORNING, SARA GAVE THE LIMO PARKED AT THE curb a curious look, as she walked toward the storefront office of Street View, the weekly paper and daily blog that she owned.

She was carrying a cup of coffee, which she switched to her left hand in order to grab her keys to unlock the door, but before she could bring them out, her partners, Emily and Amy Sharpe, opened the door and greeted her with smiles.

"Good morning, Sara, you have a visitor," Emily said.

Sara walked in and saw Johnny Rossetti seated on the sofa in the office's reception area.

Johnny gave her a smile and Sara looked at Emily and Amy. "Are you two okay?"

"Yes, he's been a perfect gentleman," Emily said.

Amy leaned in and whispered. "He might be a criminal, but if he were any hotter, I'd climb up into his lap."

Sara smiled, then, whispered back. "He is sexy, isn't he? He's also just as dangerous."

When Sara approached him, Johnny stood in greeting and offered his hand.

"Sara Blake, how are you?"

"I'm surprised by your presence here, that's how I am."

Johnny pointed toward her coffee cup. "I hope that doesn't mean you've already eaten breakfast, have you?"

"Actually, no, just the coffee."

"Good, I was hoping you would join me for a meal."

"Why?"

Johnny shrugged. "Just talk."

"We could do that here."

"I'd rather talk in private."

Sara studied him for several seconds, before turning and looking at Emily and Amy.

"I'm going for a ride with Mr. Rossetti. If I'm not back soon, call the police."

Johnny laughed. "Very dramatic."

Sara walked toward the door. "Let's go."

~

FIVE MINUTES LATER, THEY WERE IN THE REAR PARKING LOT OF A McDonald's and Johnny's driver, Mario, was passing back a bag with breakfast sandwiches in it.

Sara shook her head. "This is your idea of taking me to breakfast?"

Johnny thanked Mario and raised the mirrored divider between the seats.

"As I said, I wanted to speak to you alone, and you did place me on a time limit."

Sara took a bite of her breakfast sandwich and grinned.

"This is damn good, now what's on your mind?"

"You, you're on my mind."

"In what way?"

"In more ways than one, but for now, I'll just bring up business. That story you published about Frank Richards wasn't the smartest thing you could have done."

"Our lawyers assured us that we didn't libel the man. My

blog post only raised certain questions concerning him and MegaZenith."

"Frank Richards is not a man you want to annoy."

"Is that what this meeting is about? Richards sent you to warn me off?"

"Richards doesn't know we're meeting. This is me looking out for you."

"Why?"

Johnny reached over and touched her on the cheek. "I like you, Sara, ex-Fed or not."

"Thank you for the warning, but I can handle myself."

Johnny lowered his hand from her face and gazed into her eyes.

"Go out with me tonight."

"For what, Big Macs?"

Johnny laughed. "I was thinking of something a little fancier."

She shook her head. "I'm not looking to date anyone, least of all a mobster."

"Is that what you see when you look at me, a mobster?"

"That, and a man, a very handsome man."

Johnny leaned in and they kissed, but Sara ended it quickly.

"I'd like to go back to my office now."

Johnny sighed and hit a button on his armrest. He had to hit it twice, as Mario was lost in thoughts of concern over his FBI problems. After a moment passed, there was static, followed by the sound of Mario's voice.

"What's up, boss?"

"Take us back to Street View."

"You got it."

The intercom cut off with more static and Johnny looked over at Sara.

"If you ever change your mind, you know where to find me."

"Yes, at your club, surrounded by naked women."

"They're not really naked, and it's just a business to me."

"I see, you prefer women who keep their clothes on?"

Johnny's eyes flowed over her. "I didn't say that."

When they arrived back at Street View, Sara told Johnny to stay in the limo and that she would walk alone to the door.

"I hope to see you again, Sara."

"You never know, Mr. Rossetti."

"Call me Johnny."

"All right, Johnny, and anytime you want to tell me what you know about Frank Richards, I'll be ready to listen."

"Well hell, we could do that over dinner."

"Is that a bribe?"

"Not really, the safest thing for you would be to forget all about Frank Richards."

All trace of good humor left Sara's face.

"If what I believe is true, Richards ordered the hit that sent Tanner to kill someone I loved."

After saying that, she watched Johnny closely, searching his eyes as she asked a question.

"Does the name Brian Ames mean anything to you?"

Johnny's eyes shifted upwards and to the left, as he tried to recall the name.

"I never heard it before that I recall. Why? Is that the person you lost?"

"Yes."

"So, this is all very personal for you?"

"Of course it is."

"Be careful, Sara, Richards is a snake."

"And you work with the man, so what's that make you? Goodbye, Mr. Rossetti, and thank you for breakfast."

Sara left the limo and marched toward her office, as Johnny watched her go. She was just about to close the door behind her when she saw Johnny leave the limo.

When he reached the door, she stepped back outside.

"Yes?"

"Al Trent, you want to talk to Al Trent. He could tell you things about Richards that no one else can."

"Al Trent? Who is he?"

Johnny smiled. "He's a nerdy little prick that used to be Richards' right-hand man, that is, until he was arrested on two counts of murder."

"He's in prison?"

"No, he's out on bail, but if I had to guess, he'll either make a run for it soon, or try to cut a deal."

"A deal that involves Frank Richards? You're saying that Al Trent knows what skeletons are in Richards' closet."

Johnny wagged a finger. "I've said enough, goodbye Sara."

He had reached the limo again, when she called his name.

"Johnny!"

"Yeah?"

"Thank you."

"You just be careful."

She smiled. "Of snakes?"

"Uh-huh."

"Maybe you're not one of them after all."

Johnny spread his arms. "What you see is what you get."

He then climbed back into the limo and disappeared behind the tinted glass.

10
IT'S TIME TO GET BACK TO WORK

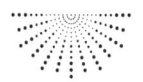

THERE WAS A MEETING LATER THAT MORNING AT THE CLUB, WITH all the Giacconi lieutenants in attendance, and Johnny let them know that Joe Pullo was the new Underboss, while he had been demoted to Consigliere.

The news surprised no one, as it had leaked the previous day, but one of the senior men stood up and spoke to Pullo.

"I'll follow you just like I followed Johnny, but from what I hear, this came down from Frank Richards, is that right?"

"It is," Pullo said.

"Yeah, well pardon my French, but that's bullshit. Who the fuck is Frank Richards to tell us how to run the Family?"

Johnny and Joe traded glances. This was exactly the sort of sentiment they wanted to hear, but for now, it had to be quelled. Johnny raised a hand to silence the men.

"We're part of The Conglomerate and Frank Richards is high up in the organization, so that's that. More importantly though, is what happened here last night."

They then discussed the attack on the club the night before and the belief that someone in the Calvino Family might have been behind the attempt. The men agreed that they would keep an eye out and then they celebrated Pullo's rise to power, while Johnny stayed in the office.

When the men left, Pullo joined Johnny.

"I could get used to running things, everybody was kissing my ass."

"Wait until we hold the formal announcement with the rest of the families, you've never seen so much ass kissing."

"Saul Adamo will be there?" Pullo said.

"Probably."

"Hmm, I say we bring more men than normal, just in case."

"I'll take care of it."

"How about that guy Romeo from last night?"

"I got him working on something else."

"What's he like?"

"He looks like a flake, but he kept his nerve last night and saved the club."

"I look forward to meeting him," Pullo said.

There was a knock on the door, and when Johnny yelled, "Come in," Merle and Earl entered.

"You wanted to see us, boss?" Merle said, but then he looked at Joe. "I mean, bosses."

Johnny smiled. "Joe's the boss now, just call me Johnny, and yeah, I wanted to see you."

Pullo stood. "I've got someplace to be for a while," Pullo said and Johnny knew that he meant he was going to visit Sam Giacconi.

"When you get back, start using the limo, it's yours now."

Pullo shook his head. "This is going to take some getting used to."

Once Pullo left, Johnny looked over at Merle and Earl.

"It's time to get back to work, boys."

"You want us to steal some cars?" Earl said.

"Hell no, you boys are more valuable than that. We need you to take care of a little problem."

Johnny passed them a file that contained a photo of a man

with a wide, florid face. Atop the picture was written a name and address.

"That's Matthew Burns; make sure he leaves the planet."

"You mean kill him?" Merle said.

"You whacked Tanner, so Burns should be a piece of cake, but you have to make it look like an accident."

The brothers gave each other a stricken look. They hadn't killed Tanner, they hadn't killed anyone, but they couldn't tell Johnny that.

"What did this guy do?"

"He's a thief. He embezzled money from the wrong people years ago, and was spotted just the other day in Jersey. You two are going to make sure he finally pays for it."

Merle looked down at the photo and thought that Burns looked like a nice guy.

"How much time do we have?"

"The sooner the better, and remember, it has to look like an accident. Don't go blasting him to pieces like you did with Tanner. We don't want the cops involved."

The boys left the club and sat in their car.

"What are we gonna do, Merle? I don't want to kill anybody."

"Me either, but if we don't kill this guy, Johnny might kill us."

"Let's go home. Let's just go back home to Arkansas and become farmers like Daddy."

"They would find us there, Merle. They would send somebody like Tanner after us and we'd be dead, instead of this guy Burns they want us to kill."

"You're right, so what do we do?"

"Let's go find this guy and see what's what."

"And then?"

"I don't know."

Earl started the engine. "If we could find Tanner we could ask him to do it, he kinda owes us."

"Maybe, but who the hell knows where he is?"

"If we get out of this, I think we should get real jobs."

"Like what?"

"I don't know, but we could start a business with the hundred grand we got."

"And what happens if they find out Tanner is alive?"

"Right, I forgot. Damn Tanner, he screwed us good."

"Why don't we just do it?"

"You mean kill the guy?"

Merle nodded. "Yeah, there's two of us and only one guy. We can do it."

"You really think so?"

"I don't know, but I guess we'll find out."

11
FIGHT OR FLIGHT?

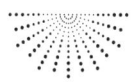

SOPHIA VERONA WATCHED IN AMAZEMENT AS THE MAN POINTING the gun at her suddenly sprouted a hole between his eyes, and she realized he'd been struck with a bullet, as the sound of the gunshot echoed throughout the house.

Sophia was on her knees with her hands bound behind her back. She wisely fell forward, to lay flat on her stomach, as the other two men spun around to face their attacker.

When she looked over her shoulder, Sophia saw a man with mirrored sunglasses and spiked blond hair firing at the men who had abducted her, and the look of calm control lighting his face shocked her.

The man displayed no fear, and Sophia knew that his shots had been on target, because the remaining two men fell beside her on the floor, and both had fatal head wounds like the first man; also like the first man, they never got off a shot.

"There's a driver in the van outside," Sophia said.

"He's toast," Tanner said and after taking out a knife, he cut Sophia's hands free and helped her to her feet. She was wearing a white blouse beneath a blue sweater, with a matching blue skirt that was short and showcased her long, shapely legs, while her red hair hung loose about her shoulders.

They were in an abandoned house on Staten Island. The Calvino Family ran the island and they were the smallest of the five Families, however, thanks mainly to Sophia's skill at Internet crime, they were third in earning power.

"Who are you?" Sophia took off the blood-spattered sweater and spoke in a breathless voice, as her heart raced. It was just seconds earlier that she thought herself about to die.

"My name is Romeo. Johnny R sent me to look out for you."

"Johnny? Oh, God bless him, and you too, Romeo. You saved my life."

Tanner pointed at the first man he'd shot. "He's one of yours, isn't he?"

"His name is Anthony Cello. I grew up with the son of a bitch. He said he'd make it quick, as if he was doing me a favor. He also told me that he was killing me on orders from Saul Adamo."

Tanner headed toward the hallway that led to the rear of the house.

"We have to leave in case somebody heard those shots."

Sophia reached down and took the weapon that seconds earlier had been aimed at her face. She and Tanner left the home, traveled through sparse woods, and climbed inside the car Tanner had left there.

"Were you following me?" Sophia asked.

"Keeping watch, and I saw them grab you off the street."

"The bastards were good, they clamped a hand over my mouth and I couldn't even scream. One second I was walking back to my car and the next thing I knew, I was in their van getting my hands tied behind my back."

"Rossetti said to protect you, but as long as Adamo is alive it sounds like you're screwed."

"If you're thinking of killing Saul, you're crazy. He'll have a dozen men around him."

"Where at? Do you know the layout, where the men will be?"

Sophia thought about it and realized that she did know where Adamo was, or rather, where he would soon be.

"Saul owns a restaurant in Staten Island. He gets there mid-morning and stays until closing. He won't have a dozen men with him, but he will have at least three or four."

"There will be staff there too?"

"Yeah, a few, but only in the kitchen. The restaurant is more like a private club for members of the Family and usually only serves dinner."

Tanner had been contemplating taking the fight to Adamo, but realized, that as Romeo, he'd be more likely to just follow orders, take Sophia to a safe place and let Johnny Rossetti worry about the rest.

"It's up to you, baby. I'm just a hired gun. Say the word and I'll take you someplace to hide until Rossetti can come get you."

Sophia stared at him as he drove along. "Hide?"

"Yeah, or I can take you straight to Rossetti."

Sophia's fear had passed, to be replaced by anger.

"Saul Adamo had a hand in killing my father, I know he did, and now he tries to kill me too. I'm not going to hide and I'm not going to run to Johnny, I'm going to take the bastard out."

"Do you have men you can trust?"

Sophia looked down at her hands, which were massaging her wrists, as she tried to get circulation back into her fingers.

"I would have said the man back there, the one who was about to kill me, was someone I could trust, but now, I'm not really sure about anybody."

"It sounds like you're on your own."

Sophia laid a hand on Tanner's bare shoulder, near the seam of his leather vest.

"What about you? Will you help me, or do you have to get permission from Johnny?"

"I'm an independent; the only permission I need is my own."

"Romeo, killing someone like Adamo without The

Conglomerate's blessing could be a death sentence. You should know that before you help me."

"I just killed three of his men. Adamo will be looking to whack me anyway."

Sophia agreed and became thoughtful. When she did speak, it seemed to Tanner as if she were thinking aloud.

"Saul thinks I'm dead and won't be worried about retaliation. I would have just disappeared like my father. If I give him time, he'll know something is wrong. He'd expect me to go to Vic Conti, or even Johnny, then he'll gather more men around himself."

"If you want to kill him, the sooner the better," Tanner said.

Sophia reached down to the floorboards and grabbed the gun she'd taken.

"Help me kill Adamo, Romeo, and I'll give you anything you want."

Tanner's gaze left the road and flowed over Sophia, paying special attention to her shapely legs.

"I'll remember you said that."

She laughed. "Fucking men, always thinking about sex."

Then, the two of them went off to find Adamo.

12
BLOOD RED

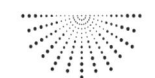

Frank Richards' bodyguard, Gary, escorted Al Trent into Richards' office with an arm on his elbow, and then guided him to sit in one of the chairs in front of the desk.

"I finally tracked him down," Gary said.

Richards studied Trent from his seat behind the desk. "You look like shit, Al."

"I feel like shit as well, sir, and let me assure you once again that I'm being framed."

Richards looked up at Gary. "Wait outside the door."

Once Gary left, Trent slid the envelope containing the pictures of Madison and Tim across the desk.

When Richards opened it, he furrowed his brow. "Madison, and who is this man? He looks familiar."

"That's Tim Jackson, the man that hacked into one of our subsidiaries and stole nearly a million dollars."

"Where did you get these pictures?"

"From a source at Tri-State Janitorial Services. Tim Jackson hacked into their system and created fake IDs for himself and Madison that allowed them to work here as part of the night cleaning crew."

"To what end?"

"To access MegaZenith's files, and if it were anyone but Jackson I would say they had no chance at decrypting them, but with a man like Jackson, who knows."

Richards rose from his seat and paced in front of the windows behind his desk.

"This could be disastrous, and Madison, to betray me this way."

"You disowned her, and she suspects you had her mother killed, which you did. Is it any wonder she'd seek revenge?"

Richards stopped pacing and stared at Trent. "You mentioned Tri-State. Does this tie-in with the murder of Carl Reese?"

"Yes, sir. I believed they framed me, or rather, Madison did, and yet, I still have no idea what happened to Jackie Verona's body and why Reese was found in its place. Perhaps Madison and Jackson were following me when Gruber committed the murder."

"Hmm, it seems my daughter has more starch than I thought. It's a pity she only utilizes it to cause me harm."

"I have a proposition, sir."

"Yes?"

"Let me track down Jackson and your daughter. It's the only way I'll clear my name, and I'm one of the few people you can trust with the files he's stolen."

Richards knew that Trent was right about the files. He had told Gary to find Trent because he had such knowledge and Richards feared that he would use that knowledge or the fact that he had ordered his wife's murder, to make a deal with the DA to avoid prison.

However, if he killed Trent now, he would still need to send someone to track down Jackson, and if Jackson disclosed how valuable the files were, he would just be trading one problem for another.

There was also the matter of motivation, something that

Trent possessed in abundance if he believed that finding Jackson would clear his name.

"All right, I'll give you all the help you need in tracking down Madison, and Tim Jackson, but I want you to do so with Gary by your side."

"Why, sir?"

"You suspect Jackson killed Reese, which means he's dangerous, but I'm sure that Gary will handle him."

"As long as he knows he's not to kill him. I'll need Jackson's testimony to prove my innocence."

"I'll make sure he knows that, but tell me, do you have any idea how to find Jackson?"

"Not a clue, but I think I know how to track down Madison."

"Ah and then she'll lead you to Jackson. Good thinking."

"My plan to find Madison involves surveillance, but if I'm correct in my assumptions, I'll have her back here in a matter of days."

"Tell Gary what's going on and he'll help you with anything you need."

Trent grinned and appeared visibly relieved as tension left his neck and shoulders.

"Thank you, Mr. Richards. I'll get those computer files back, prove my innocence, and once more take my place beside you."

Richards smiled in return and reached across the desk to shake Trent's hand.

"Good luck, son, and please, send Gary in when you're through telling him what's happening."

Trent left the office with a spring in his step, and a few minutes later, Gary returned.

"Mr. Trent said you wanted to see me?"

"Did he tell you his plans?"

"Yes, sir, we're to track down your daughter and a man named Tim Jackson."

"That traitorous bitch is no longer my daughter, but yes,

you're to assist Al with tracking her and Jackson down. Once you find them... see that they disappear."

"Sir?" Gary said, not sure if he understood what was being asked of him. Disowned or not, Madison was still Richards' flesh and blood.

"You heard me correctly; I want them both eliminated. When you find where they've been hiding, burn the place to the ground."

Gary swallowed once before speaking. "Yes, sir, and is there anything else?"

"Yes, there is, once he's no longer useful, dispose of Al Trent as well. Accomplish these tasks and I will double your salary."

Gary smiled. "Consider it done."

"You're excused," Richards said, but as Gary reached the door, he called out to him.

"Yes, sir?"

"About the girl... make certain she doesn't suffer."

"Yes, sir, I understand."

Richards watched Gary depart on a mission to kill Madison, his only child, and the last speck of white within Richards' black heart darkened to blood red.

13

A VERY SHORT LIFE

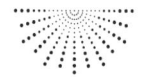

Merle and Earl were in Paterson, New Jersey, gazing out through their windshield at the home of Matthew Burns, a man they had been ordered to kill.

"Maybe we could sneak up, knock him out, and put him in the bathtub, make it look like he drowned," Earl said.

"That won't work, the cops will figure out he was hit from behind."

Earl turned in his seat and stared out the rear window.

"Let's walk back to that bar on the corner there. I need a few beers if we're goin' to do this."

"Damn right, and maybe we'll think of somethin' while we're drinkin'."

They left their car parked in front of Burns' modest home and strolled to the neighborhood pub that sat on the corner.

The lunch crowd was gathering from local businesses and the boys decided to eat as well as drink.

They sat at the bar rather than at a table. After ordering their lunch, fish and chips, they drank their first beers, trying to muster the will to do what they knew they had to do, if they wanted to keep breathing themselves.

When they were halfway through their food and on their

second beers, a man slid on the stool beside them. When Earl realized who it was, he gave his older brother a nudge.

"It's him."

Merle turned his head and found the man he was sent to kill staring at him. Matthew Burns was a large man in his mid-fifties with a red face and bright blue eyes. He had a sizable beer belly, and he towered over Merle and Earl even though they were all seated.

Burns glared at them. "I know why you two are here and let me tell you, it's not gonna happen."

∼

ON STATEN ISLAND, TANNER AND SOPHIA WATCHED THE REAR OF Saul Adamo's restaurant as a produce truck backed up to unload fresh vegetables.

They were behind a wooden fence that had seen better days, and although there was music playing from the house behind them, they were hidden from sight by the trees.

They had stopped to buy baseball caps, which they wore low, in case there were cameras, and Sophia had traded her skirt and heels for jeans and sneakers.

Tanner pointed at Sophia's gun. "Have you ever killed anyone?"

"Two guys, they were sent to kill my brother when The Conglomerate found out he was talking to the Feds. It didn't do any good, a week later, they sent Gruber and he killed him right under the Feds' noses."

"Gruber must have had a hard-on for your family."

"What do you mean?" Sophia asked, but Tanner ignored her and pointed toward the restaurant.

"There's our chance."

A member of the kitchen staff wedged open the back door to make it easier for the produce to be carted inside.

"We still don't know how many men there are?" Sophia said.

"No, but with all those empty parking spaces out front, there can't be many, and you say you know where Adamo usually sits, right?"

"He lives in that back booth. It's like his office."

"And it's right across from the entrance to the kitchen, so we go in, blast Adamo and use the produce truck to get away."

Sophia nodded. "Let's do it."

She climbed over the fence as if it wasn't there and Tanner knew she must have been a tomboy as a kid.

He followed, landed beside her, and they sprinted toward the back door with their guns up and ready. When they reached the door, they slowed, hid the guns against their sides, and walked into the kitchen as if they belonged there.

They received odd looks from the kitchen staff, but no one spoke to them or attempted to stop their progress.

Tanner went in first, cursing when he saw the empty booth where Adamo should be, and then brought up his gun to fire toward the bar, where a blond man was reaching for the piece on his hip.

Tanner hit the man twice in the side, as Sophia fired on a man behind the bar who was bringing up a shotgun.

A bald man burst from the bathroom at the other side of the large room and fired a shot that hit the wall an inch to the right of Sophia's head.

"That's Adamo!" she shouted, and Tanner took note, but he was also busy returning fire from a fourth man with a beard, who had also been sitting at the bar. He and the man missed each other, as Sophia fired a shot at Adamo that shattered the front window.

Adamo and his bearded man hid behind a corner of the bar as Tanner and Sophia took position behind a thick glass-block wall.

"You're dead, bitch!" Adamo shouted. "I've got troops headed here for a meeting."

Before the words had even left Adamo's mouth, Tanner saw two cars pull up in front as another went past and entered the alley, and he could tell by the dark shapes visible that the car held several men.

"We have to go!" Sophia said and made a move toward the doorway that led to the kitchen.

She was driven back by a barrage of gunfire delivered by Adamo and his man, and moments later, more men entered the restaurant through the shattered window, as another man shouted from the kitchen.

"Vic, me and the boys are back here, what's going on?"

Vic was Vic Conti, the Calvino boss and he answered with authority.

"Stay back there, Mikey, and don't let anybody in or out. We got a situation here."

Adamo shouted. "It's Sophia Verona. The bitch tried to kill me."

"Sophia, is that you over there? What's going on?" Vic called out.

Tanner wasn't certain which of the new men he was, but he had a rich voice that made him sound as if he were in charge, while Adamo spoke in a tone tinged with fear.

"Anthony Cello and his boys tried to kill me this morning, Vic, that's what's going on."

A mix of voices came from behind the bar, and they belonged to Vic, Adamo, and at least two other men. When the discussion died down, Vic spoke alone.

"Come out in the open unarmed and I promise you won't be hurt. You know me, Sophia. I'm not lying."

Sophia gave Tanner a strained look and then called out.

"I tried to kill Saul, I don't deny that, but it was because he tried to kill me and we both know that he had something to do with killing my father."

"That's bullshit!" Adamo called out. "I had nothing to do with Jackie going missing. He was my friend."

"Come on out, Sophia, you and whoever is back there with you, and I promise we'll listen," Conti said.

Sophia looked at Tanner. "We don't have a choice, do we?"

"Do you trust this guy?"

"I do, Vic Conti and my father were best friends, but who the hell really knows anybody?"

"We could fight, but our odds aren't good."

"I'll go first," Sophia said, then she tossed out her gun and stood with her hands in plain view.

The bearded man who had been with Adamo took aim at Sophia, but Conti slammed the butt of a gun into the side of his head, making him drop to the floor.

"Goddamn it, I gave my word she could come out. Anyone else tries to shoot her and I'll kill them," Conti said.

When nothing else happened, Tanner followed suit, but he was ready to reach for the gun he kept secured in an ankle holster.

A man Tanner took to be Vic Conti walked toward them holding a gun at his side. The man matched the voice. Conti was tall, well built, with just a bit of gray at his temples.

He scowled at Sophia. "This better be good, or I'll kill the two of you myself, understood?"

Tanner understood and wondered if Romeo was about to have a very short life.

14
INTERVENTION

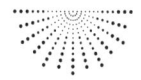

"You're salesmen, am I right or am I right?"

Merle and Earl sent Matthew Burns half-hearted smiles as they nodded in agreement.

"I knew it as soon as I saw you two get out of your car, and you can just skip my house altogether. There's been a plague of your kind around here lately, everything from driveway sealer scammers to solar power hucksters, why I've had two of your type just this week. But tell me, what are you guys selling?"

Merle looked down at himself and then over at Earl and he had to admit, the new suits did make them look like salesmen. He looked back at Matthew Burns and smiled.

"We ah, we sell life insurance."

"Whole life or term?"

"Huh?"

"What kind of policies do you sell?"

"Oh, um, all kinds, right Earl?"

"That's right, yeah, we're salesmen."

"All I need is another beer, so unless you're selling booze, I'm not interested."

Merle attracted the bartender's attention and pointed at Burn's mug.

"Bring our friend another beer, and us too while you're at it."

Once he had his fresh beer in hand, Burns raised his mug in a toast.

"You guys are all right. Hey, do you like football?"

Merle and Earl brightened at the mention of their favorite sport.

"We're Cowboys fans," Earl said.

Burns grinned at them. "Me too, but I'm a fool for the college teams. I'm a Notre Dame fan and I just love the Fighting Irish."

Merle shook his head. "We're Razorbacks fans."

"With those accents I'm not surprised. Are you boys from Arkansas?"

"We sure are," Merle said, as he and Earl settled in for an afternoon of conversation with their new friend, Matthew Burns, having forgotten all about the fact that they'd been sent to kill him.

～

Sara walked along the streets of Midtown Manhattan while keeping one eye peeled for signs of trouble. She had penned an investigative piece on Frank Richards and MegaZenith that would let the man know she had him in her sights.

Although the blog post wasn't inflammatory, it did provoke thoughts about the man's integrity and asked embarrassing questions about some of MegaZenith's dealings with other companies; in particular, it brought up the violent fate that had befallen many of the heads of its competitors. A list that seemed to stretch the bounds of mere coincidence.

While Sara wasn't looking for a violent reaction to the piece, she was hoping for a reaction. One that would grant her access to the big man himself, but so far, Richards hadn't taken the bait.

Sara arrived for her lunch date with Jake Garner and was surprised to see her sister seated beside him.

Garner stood in greeting before offering her his own seat and then he sat across from Jennifer, who was seated on Sara's right.

Jennifer leaned over and kissed her on the cheek in greeting and Sara saw the worry in her eyes.

"Don't be so nervous, Jenny. I already know about you two."

"What do you mean?"

"I happened to see you and Jake leaving a bar together yesterday, which should have you wondering why Jake would accept a lunch invitation from me today. What were you thinking Jake, that you could add another set of sisters to your scorecard?"

Garner gave her an odd look for a moment, but then he got it.

"Sara, Jennifer and I aren't sleeping together, and I thought that this lunch would be just that, two friends eating a meal together."

"Friends? Is that what we are, Jake?"

"I'd like to think so," Garner said.

Jennifer reached over and took Sara's hand. "Jake cares about you… even though you once tried to kill him."

Sara freed her hand and swiveled her head back toward Garner. "You told her about that?"

"Yes. I thought she needed to know. I thought that someone in your family should know just how obsessed and wounded the loss of Brian Ames has left you."

Sara spoke through gritted teeth to keep from screaming.

"You had no right to drag my sister into this, or to breach my privacy this way."

"You need help, Sara. I told you that when you visited me in the hospital and I still believe it's true. Tanner dying didn't cure your obsession and if I needed any proof, I found it in that blog post you wrote about Frank Richards. He's your next target, isn't he?"

"Of course he is. I believe he hired Tanner to kill Brian. Why wouldn't I go after him?"

Jennifer touched her sister gently on the cheek. "Oh baby, Jake is right, you do need help. It's not healthy to be so angry."

"Angry?" Sara said and this time her voice rose high enough to cause the nearest patrons of the restaurant to turn and look at her, while one of them, an older woman with short white hair, left the bar and walked toward their table.

"I'm not angry, Jenny. I'm fucking pissed beyond words that Brian was ripped away from me and… and I miss him. I miss him every moment of every day."

With these last words, a tear escaped, and Sara wiped it away, as the woman with the white hair sat across from her.

Jennifer gestured at the woman. "Sara, this is Dr. Whitaker. Dr. Whitaker specializes in helping people overcome depression."

Sara stared at Dr. Whitaker and saw the woman smile kindly at her.

"Hello Sara, I'm Alice Whitaker. Your sister and your friend are very worried about you and I'm here to offer my help."

Sara's mouth dropped open and she blinked in surprise as the truth hit her. She looked first at her sister and then at Garner.

"What is this, an intervention?"

Garner took her hand and gazed at her with deep concern showing in his eyes.

"I arranged all this because I care about you."

Sara freed her hand from his grip, grabbed her purse, and rushed from the restaurant as if it were on fire.

15

HUNGER KNOWS NO FEAR

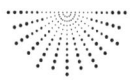

On Staten Island, Tanner sat beside Sophia in the second-floor office of a warehouse, where the various parts from stolen vehicles were housed, before being shipped overseas.

They weren't cuffed, but Tanner had been stripped of his gun, along with the weapon in the ankle holster. There were six men in the office with them, while more were scattered throughout the warehouse.

Vic Conti had listened to their stories before hearing Adamo's plea of innocence and Tanner could tell that there was little love lost between Vic and Adamo.

"They got no proof that I did shit," Adamo said.

Conti looked at Sophia with a sad expression showing. "Saul's right, Sophia."

"What are you talking about? What about the crew he sent to kill me?"

"Tony Cello is the one who's dead," Adamo said. "And I don't know anything about that."

"Sammy Vega tried to rob Johnny R's strip club last night, but he got killed for his trouble. Did you send him there?"

"The Giacconi Family are our brothers. Why would I send Vega to rob them?"

"What about my father? I bet you know what happened there, don't you?"

Adamo walked over and leaned down until his face was an inch from Sophia's.

"You got nothing but maybes, girlie, and that's not gonna save you and your friend here."

"Back off, baldy," Tanner said.

Adamo laughed at him. "Look at this guy. He looks like a clown. Is this the best you could do for a man, Sophia?"

"He was man enough to save my life and man enough to try to help me take you out."

"How'd that work out for you, huh? Vic, enough talk, hmm? It's time Sophia paid."

"If it's proof you want, I know where you can find it," Tanner said.

"What are you talking about?" Conti said.

"There are two guys over in Jersey City that have been running their mouths off about how they helped Lars Gruber waste some guy for Adamo. They said they took him to an old box factory. Now that I know Sophia's father is missing, I think maybe they were talking about him."

Tanner had heard no such thing, but he had been there when Gruber killed Sophia's father, Jackie Verona, and had later had Tim trace the license plate of the two punks that had delivered him for slaughter.

Tanner gave them the name and address and Conti sent three guys to check it out.

"The punk is just stalling," Adamo said, but his face had gone pale.

When he headed for the door, Conti called him back.

"No one goes anywhere, no one makes a call, not until this shit is settled."

Adamo puffed out his chest.

"This is how you treat your new Underboss, Vic?"

"Jackie is still the Underboss, Saul. That is, unless you know something I don't."

"I know that when a guy disappears it's not good, and with Jackie gone, I'm next in line. Frank Richards said so."

"Fuck Frank Richards," Conti said, and took out his phone.

Adamo pointed at him. "I thought you said no calls?"

"Relax, I'm ordering pizza, we could be here for a while."

"Let me call my restaurant and have them send some food over."

"Pizza will do just fine. Sophia, you want sausage on yours?"

Sophia glared at Adamo. "I'll take it plain, there's enough pig in this room already."

"I'll take pepperoni," Tanner said. "And how about some beer too?"

Conti smiled at him. "You're not scared, are you?"

"No, I'm hungry."

Conti laughed. "You're a trip, Romeo. I see why Johnny sent you to help Sophia, and I really hope I won't have to kill you."

"That makes two of us," Tanner said, and then he went back to thinking of ways to escape.

∼

GARNER CAUGHT UP TO SARA WHEN SHE WAS A BLOCK AWAY FROM the restaurant and grabbed her arm to make her stop walking.

"Let go of me!"

"No, you're going to listen to me even if you refuse to speak with the doctor."

Garner guided her into the doorway of a shoe store and placed a hand beneath her chin.

"I care about you, Sara, and that's the only reason I spoke to your sister about why you left the Bureau."

"Is that really the only reason?"

"I don't know what you mean."

"Please, Jake, I've seen the way my sister looks at you and I know what you're like. Have you bedded her?"

"The answer is no, and this has nothing to do with sex. Damn it, Sara. I'm worried about you. Frank Richards may be every bit as dangerous as Tanner was."

Sara searched his face.

"You know something, don't you? Is the Bureau going after Richards?"

"Forget Richards and come back to the restaurant with me; Jennifer is worried about you."

"I'm not talking to a shrink and you can tell Jenny that too."

"Please, think about getting help. It's not normal to be as obsessed as you are."

"What you call obsession I call justice, and I'll see to it that everyone responsible for Brian's death pays."

Garner shook his head sadly and watched as Sara strode away.

16

MARY ANN, OF COURSE

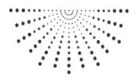

Mario was leaning against the side of the limo and smoking a cigar when Joe Pullo tapped him on the shoulder.

Mario was so startled that the cigar fell from his grasp and hit the ground.

"Why so nervous, Mario?" Joe asked. "You got problems?"

"Ah, it's nothing, boss; just a thing with my daughter, but it'll be all right."

"What's wrong with Maria?"

"It's nothing, just a problem at school."

"Okay, but keep an eye out. The trouble we had at the club might not be the last of it."

Mario nodded and opened the door for Pullo. He was a nervous wreck and had been ever since the FBI had interrogated him.

He had managed to bullshit and give them just enough to hold them, but they'd be back, and the next time they'd want much more. They might even ask him to wear a wire.

He'd heard about snitches in the past, some who had even been moved into the Witness Protection Program.

Mario always thought he'd rather squat and feed his balls into a meat grinder than rat on his friends. He also didn't want to be shipped off to some Podunk town and pretend to be someone he wasn't.

No, he didn't want to be a snitch, but if he didn't do it, his daughter would be the one to pay.

"Take me back to the club, Mario," Pullo said.

"You got it, boss."

"Just call me, Joe; I've known you since high school."

"No, I'll call you boss now; I did it for Johnny and I'll do it for you."

"Whatever," Pullo said.

Mario studied him in the rearview mirror. He and Joe had always gotten along. Maybe he should come clean, tell Joe what happened and see if he and Johnny could think of a way to get him out of the mess he was in.

Mario opened his mouth and then shut it.

What if they just killed him? It would be the simplest thing to do. Just kill him and let the FBI go find another snitch.

Mario wiped cold sweat from his brow.

A snitch for the FBI? Me?

Mario had a sudden vision of himself sitting in court and pointing at his friends, as the FBI played a bunch of recordings he made while wired up.

That bitch FBI woman, that Michelle Geary, Mario wanted to kill her for using his daughter the way she did. Maria was a good girl who had nothing to do with drugs and Geary would ruin her life just to get to him.

The thought turned Mario's fear to anger and he was blinded by rage, which is why he didn't notice that the light had turned red and drove the limo into oncoming traffic.

There was the blaring of horns, the thunder of a crash, and then for Mario, everything went black.

∼

In New Jersey, Merle and Earl laughed at the latest of Burns' stories and called for yet another pitcher of beer.

The lunch crowd had cleared out and the brothers and Burns had moved their happy trio to a corner booth.

When the beer came, the three men refilled their mugs.

They drained their mugs quickly and Merle was about to call for another pitcher when Burns invited them back to his house, where he said he had better booze.

"I want whiskey and they'll rob you blind for it here. Follow me home and we'll put on a ball game, and maybe later on I'll grill some burgers."

Merle and Earl followed happily along with their new best friend, as the three of them argued over who was hotter, Mary Ann or Ginger.

∽

At the club, Johnny shook Robert Vance's hand and then told Frank Richards' new assistant to have a seat in front of the desk.

"What did you think of the girls out front?"

Vance smiled. "I had my fill of strip clubs while I was in college. These days I like to be more hands on with women."

Johnny laughed. "I hear you. So, is this a social call or did Richards tell you to come by and check on things?"

"Both, but I'm no snitch."

"Al Trent was, that weasel looked for any opportunity to mess with me."

"As I'm sure you know, Mr. Trent has his own problems to deal with."

"Yeah, but what's your story, Vance? How did you wind up in The Conglomerate?"

"I'm ambitious, without morals, and crave power. Why are you in the Mafia?"

"Pretty much the same, and it is the family business, so to

speak," Johnny said. "But there is shit I won't do. It's a limited list, but still, there are lines I won't cross."

Vance nodded in understanding. "While I have no morals, I do have rules, and like you, I never break them."

There was a knock on the door and Carl appeared with a tray containing two glasses. He handed one to Vance and the other to Johnny.

"Anything else, boss?"

"That's it, unless Vance wants something to eat."

Vance declined food and Carl left with the empty tray.

Johnny looked across the desk at Vance. "You work for Richards; how would you also like to work for me, or is that against your rules?"

Vance smiled. "It depends, what would you want me to do?"

"I want you to be my eyes and ears at MegaZenith."

"As I said earlier, I'm no snitch."

"All right, but for your own good, keep an eye on Richards. He may look Harvard, but he's as dangerous as any street punk."

"I'll keep that in mind," Vance said and then he downed the last of his drink and stood.

"Leaving?"

"Yes, and thanks for the drink and the warning, although I already was well aware that Frank Richards is a man who cares only for himself."

Johnny wagged a finger. "It's not nice to talk about your boss that way."

Vance smiled. "I guess the drink loosened my lips, next time I'll just have coffee."

After opening the door, Vance spoke over his shoulder.

"Richards has something planned for the upcoming meeting of the ruling council and given the man he is, I can't imagine it's anything good."

"Any details?"

"No, but he's been very hands-on with that project and he's

normally a man who likes to delegate, which tells me he's hiding something."

"I'll have that coffee waiting for you the next time you drop by, along with an envelope filled with appreciation."

Vance nodded without looking back and then closed the door behind him.

17
TALENT WILL OUT

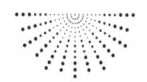

On Wall Street, inside a building named The Partners Building, Frank Richards was meeting with Saul Adamo's right-hand man, Santino.

They were inside the conference room, where The Conglomerate's ruling council was scheduled to gather on Sunday. The room was on the top floor of a ten-story building that had been renovated from the walls out. The building belonged to Richards, but his ownership was obscured behind so many layers of dummy corporations and shell companies, that it would take a miracle to discover that fact without knowing the trail to it.

Santino was the bearded man who had been with Adamo in the restaurant when Sophia and Tanner attacked.

"Where's Adamo?" Richards said.

"He couldn't make it. Jackie Verona's daughter tried to kill him."

"Was he injured?"

"No, but he had to stay and handle the situation."

Richards noticed the bandage at Santino's temple. "Were you injured?"

"I got hit on the side of the head by Vic Conti, the bastard."

Richards looked about the room in an effort to spot anything out of place. He could discern nothing except the odor of new materials, as everything in the huge room had recently been installed.

The wall-to-wall carpet was a dark blue and matched the thick curtains, which were spread open to reveal the floor-to-ceiling windows. Light from the windows illuminated the massive round conference table, a table that could seat forty. The ceiling was covered in white stucco, which was only a shade darker than the stark white walls. The black leather chairs all looked the same, because like the round table, they were chosen to keep anyone from feeling slighted, or privileged.

"How are things coming along here?"

Santino grinned. "Everything is in place; we just have to put in the new doors and test the soundproofing."

"When you do those tests, remember that not a whisper of sound can escape this room."

"I understand."

"Excellent, and since no one will be expecting trouble, things should go smoothly."

Santino laughed. "They'll never know what hit them."

~

ON STATEN ISLAND, VIC CONTI HERDED EVERYONE OUT OF THE office. They went down a long set of wooden steps and along a wide aisle to greet his men as they arrived back from Jersey City.

A man got out of the driver's seat and walked over to Vic. There was a strong resemblance to Conti in the other man's features and Tanner assumed that he was Conti's younger brother.

"They were just getting in the car when we showed up, and the second I said Jackie's name, they both turned white."

"Good work, Mikey, now let's see them."

The two bound punks were dragged from the back of a

small truck which was normally used to transport car parts, and Tanner saw that they had been worked over, as their faces were bruised, while one of them had three broken fingers on his right hand. Apparently, they hadn't come quietly.

They were the ones, the punks that had delivered Jackie Verona to that abandoned box factory, so that he could be slain by Lars Gruber.

"What did they tell you?" Conti said to his brother.

"They wouldn't talk, except to call us names."

Conti snapped his fingers in front of the punks' faces and then pointed at Adamo.

"Do you know this guy?"

The two punks stayed silent, but both sets of eyes widened in recognition.

"Look at them, they know him," Sophia said.

"What? You can read minds now," Adamo said.

One of the punks spoke up.

"Mr. Trent, that's what the German man called the guy who paid us, Mr. Trent."

"German man?" Vic said. "Are you talking about Lars Gruber?"

"I guess, but I never heard his name."

"This guy, Trent, what's he look like?"

"Young dude like me, but dressed like an old dude in a suit, and he wears glasses too."

"That's what I thought, he's Richards' assistant," Conti said.

Sophia stepped close to the men on the floor and studied them with eyes of ice.

"My father was Jackie Verona; did you kill him?"

The other punk spoke up this time and his voice was deep.

"The German dude killed him; we were just paid to help."

"But you're the ones that grabbed him off the street, right?"

"It wasn't a street; it was a restaurant."

The instant the punk mentioned a restaurant, everyone

turned toward Adamo, who was pulling a gun free from the holster on his hip.

Still unarmed, Tanner grabbed Sophia around the waist, hit the ground, and rolled beneath the truck.

A second later, Vic Conti fell to the floor with a fatal head wound and Tanner reached out and grabbed the gun from Conti's shoulder holster. Once armed, he fired at a man he knew was one of Adamo's men.

The place was chaos, and other than Adamo, Tanner couldn't be sure who was on what side, as Conti and Adamo's men battled each other, so he stayed beneath the truck and guarded Sophia.

At least, that was his plan, but Sophia slid out and grabbed a gun from one of the fallen men, to then blast at Adamo's soldiers. Tanner stood by her side and shot anyone who tried to shoot her, but when he heard the truck's engine start and the backup alarm sound off, he grabbed Sophia's waist again and pulled her toward the stairs.

It was Adamo behind the wheel. He sped backwards toward them along a wide aisle with metal shelving on both sides, as he attempted to run them down. Tanner and Sophia made it halfway up the wooden steps before the van crashed into them.

The impact destroyed the bottom part of the staircase and collapsed the handrail.

Sophia cried out in fright as she teetered at the edge, but Tanner took hold of her wrist and pulled her back onto the shuddering remains of the stairway before she could fall backwards atop the concrete floor.

"We're trapped up here," Sophia said, as the van shifted into drive and headed for the open garage door.

"We go up," Tanner said and once they reached the top, he stepped over the landing's balustrade and climbed onto the side of a metal shelf. Sophia followed his lead and the two of them climbed down the side of the metal rack, where they were met by men who had been loyal to her father.

One of them walked over with glistening eyes and a bullet wound in his arm. It was Mike, Vic Conti's brother.

"Vic's dead, Sophia. That son of a bitch Saul killed him, and you were right, he set up Jackie too."

"Did Saul get away?"

"Yeah, honey, I'm sorry, but this shit isn't over, and he can't run far enough."

"He won't run far," Tanner said. "He'll go to Richards for protection."

Mike sighed. "Damn, you're right, and Richards will back his play."

Sophia checked out Mike's arm wound. "Get that fixed and we'll figure out what we're going to do next."

Mike stared at her. "We?"

"Yes, we, or are you going to pull some macho sexist shit and pat me on the head and send me home?"

Mike studied her while he thought things over, and then gave a slight shake of his head.

"Nah, woman or not, you earned a place at the table and I'll back you on that."

"Thank you, now go see to that arm and I'll take care of the mess we have here."

"It's a mess all right, those two punks we grabbed, Saul ran them over on his way out."

"To keep them from saying any more than they did, but it won't work, and Frank Richards or not, Saul Adamo is a dead man."

Mike shook his head. "I hate to say it, but if Richards is protecting him, Saul will be damn hard to kill."

"I can take care of that for you," Tanner said, and Mike gazed his way.

"What? Are you a hit man now, Romeo?"

Tanner smiled. "You never know, I might just have a talent for it."

18

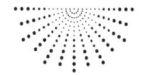

JOB PERKS

"You two got family around here, or is everyone else back in Arkansas?" Burns asked Merle and Earl, as they sat around his living room drinking whiskey.

There was a baseball game on, but the sound was muted on the huge flat screen TV.

While the outside of the home was middle-class, the furnishings were all expensive, and Merle and Earl were content in a plush blue loveseat, while Burns sat across from them on a matching sofa.

"It's just me and Earl. We got a baby sister from when our daddy remarried, but we ain't seen her since she was just a little thing. She probably don't even remember us."

Earl shook his head in disagreement. "She'd remember us, she wasn't that young, but after Daddy died, her mama married again and moved up north here."

Burns pointed at them. He was drunk, and his nose had reddened so much that it could double as a stop light.

"You boys should be glad you've got each other, it's been just me since my wife died years ago."

"Earl and I ain't never been married, but we both want to someday."

"Good luck with that, it's hard to find a real woman these days. They all want to be men."

"Some of them are all woman," Earl said with a grin, and then he told Burns about the hookers, whose services he and Merle had been gifted by Johnny.

"Where do I find this Johnny? He sounds like my kind of friend."

"He's our boss," Earl said, and the smile left his face, as he remembered why they were there.

"Your boss gives you hookers? Hell, you dudes must sell a shitload of policies, but forget about work and I'll go fire up that grill."

Burns rose from his seat and walked down the hall toward the rear of the house. As they followed along behind, Earl whispered to his brother.

"I can't hurt him, we're buddies now."

"I know, but shit, we're gonna have to do some fancy talking when we get back."

"Do you think Johnny will kill us?"

"I don't know. I just know that I can't kill Matt; like you said, he's a friend."

Burns turned around and waved them on as he entered the kitchen.

"What are you boys doing back there? Hey, grab the patties out of the fridge there, Merle, and Earl, you bring out some beer. Now, speaking of hookers, let me tell you about the time I was in New Orleans for Mardi Gras. You talk about hookers, you should have seen the one I had that day."

Burns headed out into his backyard to fire up the grill and the boys followed along happily.

∽

MARIO WOKE IN THE HOSPITAL EMERGENCY ROOM AND FOUND Pullo staring down at him.

Pullo's arm was in a sling from the gunshot wound he previously suffered, but he looked to be uninjured from the crash.

"What happened?" Mario said.

"You ran a light and we got T-boned by a truck."

"Oh no, was anybody hurt?"

"Just you."

Mario tried to sit up, but the intense ache in his skull made him change his mind.

Pullo placed a hand on his shoulder. "Lie still and I'll go get the nurse."

Pullo returned with a nurse and a doctor. After the doctor checked Mario's pupils, she smiled.

"You've suffered a concussion, but you'll be good as new soon. I also want to run a few tests. You'll be staying overnight."

Once the doctor and nurse left, Mario apologized to Pullo.

"I'm sorry as shit, Joe. I don't know what happened. Before this, I never ran a red light in my life."

"The limo is toast; I doubt we'll even get it fixed."

Mario looked at Pullo as he started to sweat. "Johnny is going to kill me… or are you going to beat him to it?"

"Yeah Mario, I'm gonna whack you because you had an accident. Relax, and whatever the hell it is that's eating you, deal with it. You can't drive in this crazy city with your mind somewhere else."

"I'll… I'll deal with it Joe, I promise."

"Good and get better quick."

Pullo left and Mario began obsessing about his predicament again.

It would have been better if I had died in the crash, he thought.

19
EASY PAYMENT PLAN

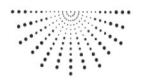

Romeo wasn't acting like Romeo and Tanner knew it, but he didn't want to play the fool in front of Sophia Verona.

One of the crew went out and bought clean-up supplies, and Tanner wore a set of white coveralls, as he helped load the bodies into the rear of a truck.

After the police failed to show, they figured that no one reported hearing gunfire and it was safe to move the bodies.

Sophia hated that they would all be buried without ceremony, but their deaths had taken place inside a warehouse stuffed with parts from the Calvino's chop shops, and on top of a murder investigation, the cops would have a field day with the thousands of stolen car parts.

Mike had taken Vic's body with him, and Sophia assumed that his family would soon have a private ceremony with the help of bribed cemetery workers.

With the grisly work done, the truck was moved, and would travel later under cover of darkness to a place where the bodies would either be incinerated or buried.

Tanner took off the blood-streaked coveralls and work gloves and tossed them in with the rest of the things burning in a trash can fire outside.

One of the men had climbed the shelving and retrieved their things from the office, and as Tanner strapped the holster on his ankle, Sophia touched him on the shoulder.

"Take me home, Romeo."

Tanner stood, nodded, and followed her out of the warehouse.

Twenty minutes later, they were parked in front of the two-story home she once lived in with her brother and father, but which now was hers alone.

Once inside, Sophia turned and hugged Tanner.

"I'd be dead if not for you."

"Can't have that," Tanner said, and Sophia kissed him on the lips.

When they separated, Sophia reached up and removed the mirrored sunglasses, then gazed into his eyes.

"I know why you wear these now. They hide the real you."

Tanner ran a hand through her long red hair. "Do you like what you see?" Tanner asked, and Sophia smiled and nodded.

"I think I promised you something for killing Adamo."

"You did, but the bastard is still alive."

Sophia took his hand and led him toward the stairs, where her bedroom was.

"We'll just have to consider this an installment then."

～

AT THAT MOMENT, ADAMO WAS MEETING WITH RICHARDS INSIDE a limousine traveling along the West Side Highway. Richards was not a happy man.

"I told you not to make any moves before the meeting, and now I learn that you not only attempted to rob that strip club, but you also bungled an attempt to kill Verona's daughter."

"The bitch was riling people up; she kept claiming that I had her father killed."

"You did."

Adamo shrugged. "Yeah, but she needed to shut up about it."

Richards let out a sigh and gazed out at the gray water of the Hudson River. When he looked back at Adamo, he had calmed down.

"You need to hide until this meeting takes place. Afterwards, I'll appoint you leader of your family, then later, I'll place you in charge of all the families, but from what I'm hearing, you have a civil war on your hands."

"Sophia Verona needs to die."

"What about your man, Santino, why not send him to kill her?"

"That's a good idea, but he'll need backup. Sophia has found herself a bodyguard named Romeo, he's also the same asshole that screwed up the robbery of the club last night."

"Not that I condone it, but the robbery of the club did have merit, and the fact that it went bad was unfortunate. After the money and guns were planted in his apartment, it would have been a perfect way to not only place Johnny Rossetti in legal difficulty, but it also would have turned his own people against him."

"It won't matter once the meeting is over, but Romeo has to go down for interfering in my business."

"Romeo? That can't be his real name, can it?"

"I don't know. He looks like a clown, but he's a stone-cold killer."

"Why do you say he looks like a clown?"

"He's got tattoos up and down both arms, spiky blond hair, and wears a leather vest with these tinted, or I guess you'd call them mirrored, sunglasses."

"He sounds charming but send Santino alone. If he succeeds, that's fine, and if he fails, well then, we've one less person that knows our plans."

Adamo laughed. "Richards, you were born on the wrong

side of the tracks. You look WASP, but you would have felt right at home in the Bronx, where I grew up."

"You're correct; I would thrive in any environment."

They arrived back at the truck Adamo had taken from the warehouse during his escape. He stepped from the limo and leaned back in to speak to Richards.

"I have a place to lie low and I'm not coming out until after the meeting."

"We're very close to getting what we want, so be careful."

Adamo sent Richards a wink and then climbed back into the truck. On the seat beside him was a hastily packed suitcase.

Richards' limo headed off toward Midtown and Adamo soon followed the same path; however, he was headed for the Holland Tunnel and his safe house in New Jersey.

~

Sara got down on her knees and placed flowers atop the grave of Brian Ames, as tears flowed freely from her eyes.

"Hello, baby."

The words were squeezed out of her from a throat constricted by grief, but she gathered herself together, for there was more she needed to say.

"Tanner is dead, Brian, not by my hand as I'd hoped, but the bastard was sent to hell all the same."

The sound of several car doors opening and closing broke her from her thoughts, and when she looked up, she saw a young family headed toward a grave on the opposite hill, where they were likely paying their respects to an elder relative who had passed away.

They were not like her, she, who visited the grave of a young man who was robbed of decades of life, and in his passing, dissolved a piece of her soul.

After watching the family for a few moments, she spoke again.

"My ex-partner and my sister, Jenny, they believe that I'm sick, that I'm suffering from depression over your loss and masking it with anger, with thoughts of revenge."

Sara made a small shrugging motion. "Maybe they're right. I thought Tanner's death would alleviate at least part of the suffering I feel over your loss, but no, it hasn't changed a thing and you're still gone."

More tears flowed, and she wiped them away.

"The bastard that sent Tanner to kill you is still alive, but unlike that animal Tanner, Frank Richards has cloaked himself in respectability and lives his life in luxury. I'm not going to kill him, Brian, but I do plan to strip him of everything he holds dear… just as he did to me."

Sara grew quiet and became lost in thoughts of Brian, even as she ached from the fact that her memories and her time spent with him were so brief and precious.

Laughter came from the other hillside, where the family was making their way back to their car.

Sara turned her head and watched them with envy, for although they had suffered loss, they still had each other to love and to laugh with, and once sorrow for their loss was expressed, they went back to the business of living.

Yes, she envied them, because she saw no life outside of one where she sought vengeance and doubted that she would ever find peace, even after its attainment.

20
TOO LEGIT TO QUIT

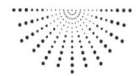

Saul Adamo's man, Santino, put away his phone after speaking with his boss and receiving new orders.

He was to find Sophia Verona and her bodyguard and kill them, and he was to do this by himself, because to bring in anyone else might result in more trouble.

Bullshit! Santino thought.

He was being sent off alone to kill two armed and dangerous people, because regardless of the outcome, Saul Adamo would win.

Saul Adamo, who was hiding like a child in the one place he thought no one could find him.

Santino knew his days were numbered when Adamo first told him what the meeting was all about, but he hadn't believed that Adamo or Richards would try to kill him until after that day had passed.

Well, it looked like he was wrong, just as Adamo was wrong in thinking that no one knew where he was.

Santino was parked at the St. George Ferry Terminal on Staten Island, and was seated atop the hood of his car, a black Mustang, while watching the lights come on in the towers of New York City, as darkness approached.

And as he sat there in the dawn of a new night, he came up with a plan of his own.

~

Merle and Earl couldn't remember when they had laughed so much, as Matthew Burns regaled them with his endless stories and encyclopedic knowledge of college football.

They had eaten charcoal-grilled burgers out on Burns' patio, drank more whiskey, and then moved back inside the house to watch sports.

"Boys, I can't remember the last time I enjoyed myself so much," Burns said.

"Us too, but if Earl and I drank like this every day, we'd regret it," Merle said.

"I do have a talent for it, don't I?" Burns said, and then he drained another glass of whiskey.

He refilled his glass, but when he went to do the same with Merle's, he was waved off.

"No more, thanks, we gotta drive back to the city."

"Screw that, Merle. You boys can camp out here on the sofa and the recliner. Hell, I've passed out in that chair more nights than I care to admit, but it's comfortable as hell."

The brothers exchanged glances and shrugged.

"I guess we're stayin,'" Earl said, and Burns poured more whiskey.

~

Although they had showered together before making love, Tanner and Sophia showered again separately before leaving her house to find Adamo.

Tanner had been concerned that the fake tattoos would run beneath the spray of water, but they were of top quality and had held up.

He really hadn't expected to be playing Romeo for as long as he had, but events had carried him along and he had let them.

After leaving Sophia's, they went to Adamo's apartment, where Tanner was impressed with how quickly Sophia disabled the alarm.

"If it's electronic, I'm its master. You should see me when I'm hacking on the computer."

"You remind me of a guy that I know."

Sophia looked at him askance. "I remind you of a guy?"

"In skill set only," Tanner said.

The apartment was a bust as they assumed it would be, but there were signs that Adamo had packed in haste before leaving.

"What if he's flown off somewhere?" Sophia said.

"He could have, but I doubt it, not with Richards backing his play. It's more likely that he'll send someone to kill us and then emerge from his hiding place."

"If anyone is hunting us, it's Santino, the bearded man who was at the restaurant this morning."

"I remember him, and the restaurant is the next place we look."

"Adamo wouldn't hide there, it's even more obvious than here," Sophia said.

"It's obvious, but we have to check."

∼

THEY ARRIVED AT THE RESTAURANT AND FOUND THE LIGHTS ablaze, while the window that had shattered earlier had been replaced with plywood.

They entered through the back, while being wary of an ambush. However, when they made their way through the kitchen and into the restaurant, the only thing they found waiting for them was a note, which had been placed atop a stool on a clipboard.

In block letters written with a marker, it gave the address in New Jersey where Adamo could be found.

Sophia appeared puzzled. "Are they trying to lead us into a trap?"

"It could be a trap, or maybe Santino has become sick of his boss and figures he'll use us to retire him," Tanner said.

"I guess we visit New Jersey."

"Yeah and if this is legit, Adamo is about to become a permanent resident there."

21
ONE MAN'S LOSS

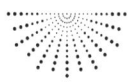

"There's a guy out here to see you, Johnny, says his name is Vance."

Johnny Rossetti looked up from the pile of food and beverage invoices on his desk and spoke to the man with the scar standing in the doorway, as loud music rushed in from the club.

"Send him in, Bull, but frisk him first."

"You got it."

The door closed, and the pounding beat went to a fraction of what it was, until seconds later, the door opened again, and Robert Vance stepped in wearing a smile, as he tossed a thumb back toward the club.

"I may have been premature in saying I've outgrown strip clubs, there's a brunette on stage right now that I could watch dance all day."

"Her name is Skye and she'll dance for you in private if you've got three bills to spare."

"Three hundred dollars for a lap dance?"

"She's the best and gets more requests than anyone. If I had to guess, I'd say she's got a little money put away, but you didn't come back here so soon to talk about my dancers. What's up?"

Vance smiled. "I'll get to that, but I believe you said something about coffee the last time we spoke."

Johnny chuckled. There was a table in the left-hand corner, with a small refrigerator parked between its legs, while atop it sat a coffeemaker. Johnny went to it and poured coffee into a black ceramic mug. After returning to the desk, he reached into the top drawer, took out an envelope and sat it in front of Vance, but only after placing the coffee cup on top.

"There's creamer in the mini fridge, but there's sugar in that envelope."

Vance moved the cup aside, and after looking into the envelope, he stuck it in the side pocket of his jeans.

"Very sweet, and money well spent, because I'm here to tell you that Richards is setting you up for something."

"What makes you say that?"

"It's a feeling I get every time I hear him dog you to someone. He was on the phone earlier, making calls, and he mentioned you in every conversation. I heard him say, 'Johnny Rossetti can't be trusted,' or 'Johnny Rossetti is furious over his demotion and I'm afraid he'll do something to get back at us.' Words like that, as if he were priming everyone to expect the worst from you."

Johnny rubbed his chin as he thought things over. "I'll keep both eyes open and the next time Richards wants me to go left, I'll head right."

Vance rose from his seat. "It's getting late, and I'll keep you posted."

"Do that, but watch your back, like you said earlier, Richards cares only for himself."

"Until next time," Vance said, and then he left.

Johnny picked up his phone and dialed Bull. "The guy that's leaving the office, have one of your boys follow him."

"You got it," Bull said.

"One more thing, didn't I see one of our cops in the club tonight?"

"Yeah, Detective O'Leary, do you want to see him?"

"Yes, send him back here."

O'Leary arrived about a minute later. He was a middle-aged man with reddish-blond hair and gray eyes. He had been on the take since he was a rookie.

"What's up?"

The coffee cup that Vance had touched was wrapped in a plastic bag. Johnny passed it across the desk to O'Leary.

"There are two sets of prints on there, mine and someone else's. I want to know who that someone else really is."

"I assume it's a rush job?"

"You assume correctly."

"You'll have it tomorrow morning."

"Thanks, Sean."

O'Leary left, and Johnny leaned back in his seat. Maybe Vance was what he seemed and maybe not, time would tell.

∼

JAKE GARNER PLACED AN EYE TO HIS PEEPHOLE AND WAS surprised by what he saw.

He opened the door to his apartment and smiled. "Sara, this is a nice surprise."

"Can I come in?"

"Of course," Garner said. He was wearing a blue silk robe with black boxer shorts on beneath, as he had been getting ready to go to bed. As Sara passed him, he caught the scent of liquor.

After closing the door, he turned to ask her if she'd been driving, and she wrapped her arms around him and kissed him.

"Take me to bed, Jake. I'm tired of being lonely and I just want to forget for a while, for just a while."

Garner gently disengaged from Sara, but he held her by the arms as he studied her eyes.

"I think you're drunk."

"Maybe a little, but I'm not so drunk that I don't know what I'm doing."

She dropped her purse, stood on her toes and kissed him again, as one hand pressed against his chest and the other slipped beneath the robe.

Garner kissed her back as he felt her hand slide beneath the elastic of his boxers, and despite releasing a moan of pleasure, he pushed her away once more.

"No. As much as I want to, no, you don't need me to be a lover. Right now, you need me to be a friend."

Sara blinked her eyes rapidly and steadied herself. "You don't want me?"

"Not in my bed, not the way you are now. I'd just be using you."

"You don't want me? You, a man who fucks any woman with a pulse?"

Garner moved closer and caressed her cheek. "You're not just any woman to me."

Sara looked at him with horror, as an idea struck her.

"You don't want to be with me because you think I'm damaged goods, that's it, isn't it?"

"No! Yes, you have problems, you have issues, God knows, but I've never thought of you as damaged, and I've begun to hope that someday we could be more than friends."

"Liar!"

Sara headed for the door, and the swiftness of her movement made her stumble, but she regained her balance, scooped up her purse, and opened the door.

"Sara, stay and we'll talk."

"Go to hell, Jake."

She slammed the door behind her and rushed toward the elevator, which opened as soon as she hit the call button.

Garner nearly made it inside the elevator, but the doors closed before he could reach her, and Sara shouted to him just as the car began to move downward. "Leave me alone!"

She reached the lobby, looked up through tears, and saw that the other elevator was moving downward as well.

She was climbing into a taxi when she saw Garner looking at her through his apartment building's front doors; he was barefoot, with the robe hanging open and a look of concern on his handsome face.

After getting into the taxi, she told the cabbie to, "Just drive," and took a sip from the flask she carried in her purse.

"Miss, I'll still need an address."

Sara gave it some thought and smiled. "Take me to the Cabaret Strip Club."

If Garner didn't want her, she knew a man who did.

22

WOULD SMELL AS SWEET

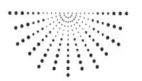

Mario woke from a bad dream only to find that waking life mirrored it.

Despite it being long after visiting hours ended, FBI agent Michelle Geary was in his hospital room and had been watching him as he slept.

"Hello Mario, you didn't think I'd forgotten about you, did you?"

Mario just stared back at her and tried not to let his hate for her show.

Geary smiled, and her chin-length blonde hair hung loosely and framed her attractive face.

If Mario had met her in a bar as a stranger, he might have tried to pick her up, but as things stood, he despised the woman for using his daughter to get to him. Geary only wanted him so she could hurt his friends.

Mario wasn't deluded; he knew what he was and what his friends were. They were men like Joe Pullo, who would kill just about anyone because he was ordered to, but despite their ruthlessness, they had rules and the rules said that family was off limits.

"How did you get in here after visiting hours?"

Geary leaned back in her seat. "I have a badge and it opens a lot of doors."

"It makes you feel big too, doesn't it?"

"When you leave the hospital, I want you to call me, and Mario, the time for talk is over. You either give me something that I can use against your bosses or I'm arresting your daughter. Do you understand me?"

Mario nodded with his teeth clenched.

"Say that you understand. I want to hear it."

"I understand."

"You'd better, or so help me I'll feed that tender young daughter of yours to those bull dykes inside the women's prison on Rikers Island. They would love to have a tasty little morsel like her."

For just a moment, Mario felt the urge to attack Geary and strangle her to death, but the moment passed, and he swallowed his rage.

"I'll give you something you can use, I promise."

Geary patted him on the cheek. "That's a good boy. Give me something I can use and your daughter's problem disappears."

Geary rose from the chair and left without another word.

Mario had spent most of his career transporting drugs, and later became Sam Giacconi's chauffeur. He was a nobody in The Giacconi Family, but he did know where the bodies were hidden, and there were two recent corpses that the Feds would love to find.

Mario stared at the ceiling, knowing that he'd never get back to sleep, and tried to think of a way to get out from under the mess he was in.

∼

TANNER STUDIED THE SMALL, BUT WELL-MAINTAINED HOME IN

the town of Union, New Jersey, even as his hand removed the lock picks from his pocket.

"We'll take our time checking it out and then we'll go in the back door. If there's an alarm system, it's yours to deal with."

Sophia nodded in agreement and they crept toward the house.

When they were satisfied that there were no guards or dogs, they entered through the rear door as planned, and after long minutes of great care expended in silent movement, they stood at the side of Adamo's bed, where he lay entwined with his lover.

Tanner picked up the gun that Adamo had left on the nightstand, gave Sophia a signal, and watched as she shined the beam of a small flashlight at Adamo's eyes.

The bald man awoke with a start as he reached for a weapon that was no longer there, and his movements awakened the young man who had been lying in his arms.

"Saul, baby, what's going on?" the young man muttered in a sleepy voice. He was probably no more than twenty.

Sophia hit him on the side of his blond head with her gun and he lay silent once more.

Adamo gave up on finding the gun and turned on a lamp. When he saw Sophia and Tanner, panic lit his face.

"How did you find me here? Who else knows about this?"

"We were tipped off," Sophia said.

"Oh God, someone knows and now you do too, oh Jesus, oh no."

Sophia looked over at Tanner with an astonished look on her face that didn't need words.

Tanner nodded. Yes, Adamo was actually more distraught about their discovery that he was gay than he was that they were there to kill him.

"Adamo, Sophia and I wouldn't care if you were fucking a mongoose. I don't give a damn who anyone fucks, I only care about who they fuck with, and you've fucked with the wrong people."

Tanner had traded the leather vest for a black T-shirt with long sleeves, but he had left the bolo tie in place around his neck.

In one smooth motion, he removed the tie and slipped it over Adamo's head.

As he had done with Gruber, he used the tie as a garrote, but to avoid the blood bath that Gruber's demise had spawned with a quick death, Tanner instead kept a steady killing pressure around Adamo's throat.

Adamo thrashed like a sport fish caught on a line. Tanner held on, dragged him from the bed, and finished Adamo as he lay on the floor. Adamo's face was a bright red that extended to his bald pate, making it appear as if he had been sunburned.

The murder took nearly three minutes. Toward the end of it, Tanner had locked eyes with Sophia, expecting to see revulsion. Instead, he saw a look of satisfaction, as she watched the man who had setup her father's murder meet his end.

When he was done, Tanner freed the bolo and stuffed it in a pocket.

Sophia gestured at the naked young man she had knocked unconscious.

"What should we do with him?"

"Leave him as he is, but we'll take Adamo's body away."

"That sounds risky."

"It is, but not as dangerous as leaving him and pinpointing the time of death. If he just goes missing, who's to say when he was murdered, or where?"

"That's the same logic they used when killing my father, and yes, it left us confused and uncertain."

"Yeah, and I doubt the kid on the bed has a clue who Adamo really was."

Adamo had bled very little, so Tanner wrapped him in a blanket and hefted him on his shoulder. Like Tanner, Sophia was wearing gloves. She walked around the bed to turn off the light.

Minutes later, they were in the home's driveway with Adamo's corpse stored in the truck he had arrived in. Tanner would drive it away with Sophia following in his car. As he was about to climb in the truck, Sophia gripped his arm.

"Romeo?"

"Yeah?"

She kissed him. "Thank you."

"You're welcome, but we need to move."

Another quick kiss and Sophia ran to his car.

Tanner climbed in the truck and headed toward the highway as Sophia drove along behind him.

In his brief existence, Romeo had killed several men; he was a lethal chap, on that score, there was no doubt.

Tanner sighed. *Oh well, a rose by any other name...*

Tanner drove on, headed back to New York City, and wondered how many more would die in the coming days.

23
ABSOLUTELY

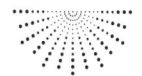

Johnny watched Sara enter the club and could tell right away that she was drunk.

He went toward her, and as he did so, he saw that one of the customers had also spotted her and the man was moving in for the kill.

"Damn baby, you must be a dancer, because you're hot as shit."

He was a young guy in a good suit, likely a stockbroker, and he was nearly as drunk as Sara. When he leaned in to kiss her, Sara shoved him backwards.

The man moved toward her again and Johnny stepped between them.

"It's time to go home."

"Screw you. I'll leave when I want."

"You want to leave now," said a voice from behind the man, and when the man turned around, he saw Bull standing behind him.

The man craned his neck to gaze up at the giant.

"I'll leave, yeah, no problem."

Sara waved at the man, as Bull escorted him to the door.

"Bye-bye." When she was done waving, she turned and smiled at Johnny. "Hello."

Johnny took her by the arm. "Let's go to my office."

"Okay, but I want a drink."

"What would you like?"

"A martini would be nice. Do you make apple martinis here?"

Johnny caught Carl's attention. "Two apple martinis and have them sent to my office."

"Right, boss."

Sara was watching the stage, where blonde twins were keeping a crowd of men six deep enraptured by their… athletic ability, as they shimmied their half-naked bodies up, down, and around a pair of shiny metal poles in synchronized splendor.

"That looks difficult to do, and they're so young and beautiful."

"You're young and beautiful too."

"Maybe beautiful, but not young, not inside."

Carl had made the martinis as they talked. Johnny took the tray from him and led the way to his office.

Sara entered, looked around, and settled on the leather sofa against the wall. Johnny sat beside her and placed the tray on the coffee table.

"Two martinis? Are you trying to get me drunk?"

"You're already there, honey, and one of those is for me."

Sara took the drink, sipped it, and smiled. "That's excellent."

"I'm glad you like it."

Sara sat the drink down and stared at Johnny. "There's something else I'd like."

She kissed him, and he kissed her back. When their lips parted, she sighed.

"You're a good kisser."

She grabbed her drink again, spilling part of it, and then gulped the remainder down.

Johnny watched her and saw a shadow of sadness envelop her.

"What's wrong, Sara?"

"My sister thinks I'm crazy," Sara said, while pronouncing "crazy" as "crazshey."

"Why would she think that?"

"She and my ex-partner think I'm obsessed with seeking revenge on the men who killed my lover."

"I thought Tanner had killed him?"

"He did, but he did it on orders and now I want the man behind him."

"Frank Richards."

Sara nodded, grabbed the second martini and downed the green-hued fluid in a series of gulps. When she was done, she burped loudly, followed it with a giggle, then leaned over and kissed Johnny again.

"I don't want to talk. I don't want to think. Just take me home with you."

Johnny looked her over as he smiled. "Absolutely."

24
MISSION ACCOMPLISHED

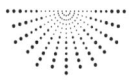

Merle awoke with a pounding headache and wondered where he was.

When he saw his brother sleeping nearby in a recliner, he remembered that they were with their new friend, Matthew Burns.

A moment later, Merle caught the scent of bacon and figured that Burns had gotten up and started cooking breakfast.

Good, because he was hungry and would kill for a cup of coffee.

Kill? Shit, if I could kill I wouldn't be in trouble. Johnny R is not gonna like it when we tell him we didn't kill Burns. Damn it, why'd Matt have to be such a nice guy?

Merle lay there a little longer, letting his eyes adjust to the daylight leaking through the blinds, as the pounding in his head became a more manageable ache.

Earl stirred and when Merle looked over at his younger brother, he saw his eyes pop open, only to squinch shut, and he knew he wasn't the only one with a hangover.

"Mornin'," Merle said.

"My head hurts."

"Me too."

Earl opened his eyes and sniffed the air. "Somethin's burnin'."

"It's just bacon, Matt's cookin'."

"Nah, somethin's burnin', you don't smell that?"

Merle gave the air a good sniff, and yes, something was burning.

He leapt from the sofa, moaned from the ache in his head, and with Earl following, headed toward the kitchen.

"Matt!"

Burns was sitting on the floor, slumped back against the bottom cabinets. His eyes were closed, but his mouth hung open, and in one hand, he gripped a rubber spatula, while the other laid atop his chest.

What had been scrambled eggs were burning in a pan, while a dozen strips of bacon blackened atop an electric griddle.

Merle got down on the floor beside Burns as Earl turned off the food.

"Oh, sweet Jesus, Matt. Matt, are you okay?"

After getting no response from Burns, Merle looked up at his brother.

"Call 9-1-1 and tell them to hurry!"

∽

On a back road near the village of Tarrytown, New York, Trent and Gary sat in a van and waited to see if Madison would appear.

They were off-road, as they had driven a hundred yards down an old dirt track barely wide enough for the van, and then into a clearing where they turned around, so they had a view of the road.

Gary didn't talk unless he was first spoken to when he was with Richards, but Trent wasn't Richards, and curiosity caused him to ask Al Trent a few questions.

"Why are we here?"

"Because this is where Mr. Richards' daughter will appear at some point today."

"Out here in the middle of nowhere?"

"Do you see that tree there on the right side of the road, the old one?"

"Yeah, it's all twisty."

"Yes, it's gnarled, and it's also the tree that Madison's mother crashed her car into on the night she died. Madison once told me that she leaves flowers here for her mother."

"Here? Why not at her grave?"

"There is no grave. Mr. Richards had his wife's body cremated and her ashes scattered."

Gary nodded. "Okay, then yeah, she might show here, but what if she doesn't come by for weeks, or months?"

"She'll be here today, because today is her mother's birthday."

"That does improve the odds, but what if she doesn't show?"

"She'll show," Trent said, while wishing he felt as certain as he sounded.

∼

MERLE CRIED, AS DID EARL, AS THEY WATCHED THE AMBULANCE ride off with the body of Matthew Burns.

An officer arrived after the ambulance came, and the young female cop was giving the boys looks of sympathy.

"If it's any consolation, the paramedics say he went quickly. He likely just felt a sharp pain in his chest and then slid to the floor where you found him."

Merle wiped at his eyes. "He was such a fun guy and he knew everythin' about college football."

"Had you been friends with him for a long time?"

"No ma'am, Earl and I just met him, but we really hit it off, ya know?"

"I've finished my report. Is there anything you need from the home?"

"No and I guess we'll head back to the city now."

"Take care, gentlemen, and again, I'm sorry for your loss."

The boys climbed into their car and drove away. Their mission accomplished, their hearts broken.

25

YOU'RE NEVER TOO OLD FOR A QUICKIE

Sara woke with a dry mouth and an urgent feeling in her bladder.

Her mind was foggy, but free of pain, and an entire minute passed before she realized she wasn't in her own bedroom.

She sat up, gazed about and felt the ache in her bladder increase. On the left side of the room was an open doorway that revealed a bathroom, and she rose from the bed and headed for it.

I was with Johnny last night.

It wasn't until she was pulling her underwear down to pee that she realized she was still dressed, and that only her shoes were missing.

She found the shoes by the side of the bed, put them on, and looked around at the room.

There wasn't much to see other than the bedroom furniture. The walls and ceiling were a muted shade of white, while the curtains and carpet were both dark blue. There was the sound of traffic outside, but it was sporadic. Sara guessed that the apartment wasn't on a main drag.

She remembered leaving the club, kissing during the short cab ride, and after that… nothing. The room had no pictures, but there was a bookcase in a corner and Sara saw with surprise that there were several books on aviation, along with books on leadership, business administration, and several classic novels.

She returned to the bathroom to wash her face and then left the room.

Johnny Rossetti was seated in a kitchen area that was separated from the large living room by a short wall, and from what she could see past the glass patio doors, Sara realized they were on an upper floor.

Johnny smiled. "Good morning, how do you feel?"

"Befuddled, did I pass out last night?"

"Yeah, right in the middle of a kiss; I guess that makes me the anti-Prince Charming."

"You carried me to your bed?"

"Yeah, and I slept on the couch."

"Some men might have taken advantage of the situation."

"I ain't one of them, honey, and don't forget, I know what you did to Vince."

"That pig tried to rape me. If anything had happened last night, I would have thought of you as a scumbag, but I would have been equally to blame by my stupidity."

"You were hurting, and you wanted to forget and be comforted, I got that, and I'm glad that you came to me."

"Is there any coffee?"

Johnny rose and poured Sara a cup as she took a seat at the table.

"This is good coffee, thank you, and thank you for last night."

"Not a problem, Sara, we all hit bottom sometime."

Sara glanced around. "There's no girlfriend, is there?"

"No."

"What am I saying, anytime you want company, you can just grab one of the girls at the club on your way out the door."

Johnny laughed. "It's not like that, not at my club. The girls dance, yes, but they're not hookers, and a few of them are married."

"So what, you're saying you order up one of your hookers instead?"

"I won't lie. I could do that, and have in the past, but I was a young punk then. Actually, the last woman I dated was a doctor, a pediatrician."

"I saw books in the bedroom on aviation, do you fly?"

"Yeah, I took it up as a hobby years ago and love it."

"My father is a pilot. He used to take me and my sister up for rides all the time. It's exhilarating in a small plane."

"I have a two-seater, a Cessna Skycatcher; let me know if you ever want to go for a ride."

"I'll do that," Sara said, and then she and Johnny just stared at each other until he finally broke the silence.

"About last night…?"

"Yes?"

"Was that a spur of the moment impulse fueled by booze, or is there a chance I'll see you again?"

"Are you sure you want to?"

"Absolutely, you're an interesting woman, Sara Blake, and more like me than you'd probably care to admit."

"You think I'm a bad girl?"

Johnny grinned. "I know you're a bad girl. I'd just like to find out how bad."

~

ON STATEN ISLAND, SOPHIA CLIMBED OUT OF BED, GRABBED HER robe, and found Tanner sitting at her kitchen table and cleaning his gun.

She kissed him. "Good morning, Romeo."

"Hello there," Tanner said. His dyed blond hair was spiked, but he wasn't wearing the sunglasses or Romeo's vest. He was tired of being Romeo and was ready to do what he came back to Manhattan for in the first place, to kill Frank Richards.

Sophia sat beside him and checked her phone for messages. "Mike called. We're having a meeting with the Family on Monday and I have to be there."

"Will that be dangerous?"

"No, but then that might depend on what happens tomorrow."

"What's going on tomorrow?" Tanner said, feigning ignorance.

"All the Conglomerate big shots are getting together, even the ones from Europe."

"Will you be going?"

Sophia laughed. "They barely know I'm alive. No, only Johnny gets to be there, but wait, I guess it's Joe Pullo now, since he's the new Underboss. Do you know Joe?"

"No, we've never met."

"I only met him once, but I know my father liked him. He'll be at the meeting for all the New York Families, like a spokesperson."

"How many people will be at that meeting?"

"I don't know, dozens I guess, and hopefully things will get straightened out. The Conglomerate was supposed to be a partnership with big business, but Frank Richards thinks he owns us."

"The mob isn't what it once was, not since the Russians and the other gangs started taking territory away."

"It's not just that, it's the Feds too, some of them are really vicious, like that bitch that used my brother."

"I heard about your brother. Are you now saying that he wasn't a snitch?"

Sophia lowered her eyes. "No, he turned, but he only did it to save our father."

"The Feds wanted Jackie Verona, but settled for his son?"

"Tony, my brother, he made a deal that they couldn't resist. He was going to give up everyone but our father."

"This Fed, you said she was a woman, her name wasn't Sara Blake, was it?"

"No, I've never heard of her. No her name was Michelle Geary, and from what Tony said, she sounds like a bitch and a half."

~

MICHELLE GEARY WATCHED JAKE GARNER AS HE PUSHED HIS plate aside with his food barely touched. They were meeting over breakfast to discuss Mario.

Technically, they had the day off, so they were both dressed casually. Garner had on jeans and a gray polo shirt, while Geary wore a white skirt that exposed her shapely legs, and her blue blouse, with the top buttons undone, displayed a freckled cleavage.

"No appetite? That means that something is eating you, what is it?"

"I was trying to help a friend and I think I scared her away."

"A woman? Since when are you friends with a woman? And don't say me, because one, we're not friends, and two, you don't like me."

"It's Sara Blake; I've been trying to help her."

Geary laughed loud enough to draw attention to their table, but she took no note of it.

"Garner, the bitch is crazy; she shot you three times and nearly killed you."

"She wasn't trying to kill me, and I don't think she's crazy. She's just hurting because she suffered a loss."

Geary sent him a knowing smile. "You want to get her into bed. I've met her and she's cute, but damn, let it go. The bitch is damaged goods."

"Don't say that!"

Garner had shouted so loudly that every other conversation stopped. He gave an embarrassed look as he gazed around and held up a hand, as if to apologize. When he looked back at Geary, she was smiling.

"Holy shit, you love the woman, don't you?"

"That's ridiculous, but yes, I care about her. But never mind Sara, what were you saying about Mario Petrocelli?"

"It looks like he's in the hospital for one more day, but I want to drop by later and rattle his chain, both of us, or aren't you working this case with me?"

"You know how I feel about your methods, but yes, I'll talk to him too. I have sympathy for his daughter, but none for him."

"Good, now tell me the truth; am I too old for you?"

"What are you asking?"

"I'm saying that you're one serious hunk of man and I want you. What do you say?"

Garner studied Geary. She was years older than he was, but she had a body that was still young, and her blonde hair sat atop a face that was more than pretty.

He stood and placed money on the table for the bill.

"I think we should keep things professional."

Geary stared up at him. "You really don't like me, do you?"

"As I said before, I don't like your methods, Michelle; as far as the offer, I was tempted."

"I won't ask again, you know where to find me, and I'll meet you at the hospital at seven."

"Fine, I'll see you then."

Garner had taken three steps when Geary called to him.

"When you see Sara, tell her I said hi."

Garner said nothing and kept walking, as behind him, Geary chuckled with amusement.

26

MINOR ANNOYANCES

Frank Richards stepped off the elevator, and after traveling the corridors along the tenth floor of The Partners Building, he found Santino waiting for him outside the meeting room. Walking beside Richards was his new assistant, Robert Vance.

"What's this about a problem?" Richards said, as he looked through the glass doors to spot anything amiss.

Santino raised up his hand in a calming gesture. "The meeting room is ready. The problem is with Saul Adamo."

"What problem is that?"

"He's dead."

Richards swore beneath his breath. Afterwards, he told Santino and Vance to turn around, so that they wouldn't see what five-letter word he tapped into the keypad that controlled the door locks.

When he was finished, the doors hissed and opened inward, which caused the lights to come on automatically.

Richards walked inside and gestured for Santino to sit. Santino did so and found Richards glaring down at him.

"What happened to Adamo?"

"He was killed by Sophia Verona and her pet, Romeo."

"The very people you were ordered to deal with."

"I decided not to follow those orders because I knew it was a setup. You two bastards were hoping we'd all kill each other, but I outsmarted you and Adamo both. Now, I'm the one who will be your partner."

"I choose my partners, Mr. Santino, not the other way around."

Santino stood in a rush, while shoving his chair backwards, then he leaned his face near Richards.

"Listen to me, you blue-blooded mobster wannabe. You and I are partners now and there's not a goddamn thing you can do about it."

Richards stiffened from the close contact, then he shifted his eyes to the left, where Vance was standing.

"Mr. Vance, I would like this problem erased."

Santino took a step back as he reached beneath his suit jacket for the gun in his shoulder holster, but he felt his hand go numb as Vance jabbed at a nerve cluster beneath his armpit. A second later and Vance knocked Santino to his knees, then moved behind him.

As this was happening, Richards had turned away to stare out into the hallway. While he was a man who ordered violent acts be committed to further his aims, he did not enjoy seeing them employed.

The sound of a struggle came from behind him. After hearing Santino grunt, Richards heard something that sounded like a thick branch snapping in two. It was Santino's neck breaking and it was followed by the sound of his body falling to the floor.

When Vance appeared beside him, Richards looked over and saw that the man had barely exerted himself.

"Is there any blood?"

"No, sir, and I'll remove the body shortly."

"Do that, I want no signs of violence detectable in this room."

"There won't be, but sir, who will you choose to take Adamo's place?"

"I was thinking of Joe Pullo. The man has a soldier's mentality and I think he would follow my orders if well compensated. However, I've grown tired of dealing with his kind. I don't need one of them to help me rule them. I'll rule them myself and they'll accept it or die, but that comes later. My focus is on tomorrow's meeting."

"I'll get together with Johnny Rossetti again too."

"He trusts you?"

Vance smiled. "Enough for our purposes. I'll lure him here tomorrow morning and complete the first part of your plan."

"Good, but remember, don't hurt him. I need him healthy if he's to play the patsy."

"I understand, sir, and I won't let you down."

"Good man, now clean up that mess and meet me back at the office. There are still a few details I want to go over."

"Speaking of details, what's to be done with Sophia Verona and this man, Romeo?"

Richards looked thoughtful as he weighed his options.

Vance spoke up. "I'd like to make a suggestion."

"Yes?"

"Why not use honey instead of vinegar? Invite the woman to the meeting tomorrow. It'll placate her long enough for your plan to work."

Richards nodded. "That's one option, but Sophia Verona and this Romeo person have been particularly annoying, and I want them eradicated. Send a team after them."

"Men from one of the other families?"

"No, use mercenaries, and tell them that they'll be paid double if it's completed before sunrise tomorrow."

"Yes, sir, consider it done."

Richards turned his head just far enough around so that he could view Santino's corpse in his peripheral vision. He grimaced when he caught a glimpse of the unnatural position of Santino's head.

He looked back at Vance. "I should have made you my assistant sooner, Robert. It's nice to have a man around who can handle… minor annoyances."

"Yes, sir, and it was my pleasure to do so."

Richards smiled and headed for the elevator, as thoughts of gaining greater power swam through his mind.

27
NYUK, NYUK, NYUK

Merle and Earl entered the Cabaret Strip Club in the afternoon and took seats at the bar to speak to Carl.

"Is Johnny here?"

"Nope, but he should be soon. You guys want a beer?"

"Just a soda for me," Merle said. "I drank enough yesterday to hold me for a week."

Earl also had soda, then they turned on their barstools and watched the young woman who was dancing for the small Saturday afternoon crowd.

Johnny appeared a short time later and the boys followed him inside the office.

"If you're here, I take it that means that Matthew Burns no longer walks among us?"

Merle nodded and fought back tears as he thought of Matt.

"Good work, and the cops will think it's an accident, right?"

"Yeah," Earl said. "They think he had a heart attack."

"They think? I'm no doctor, but a thing like that leaves tell-tale signs behind, chemical changes in the blood, that type of shit. Take a seat."

Johnny took out a phone, made a call, and asked the person

on the other line to check on the details of Matthew Burns' demise.

After ending the call, he bullshitted with Merle and Earl as he opened his laptop and signed on to check his email. A few minutes later, his call was returned. When he put down the phone, he looked perplexed.

"All right, tell me what happened."

"What d'ya mean?" Merle said.

"The dude definitely died of a heart attack, but this isn't the CIA, boys. We don't have any undetectable drugs and spy gadgets. How the hell could you induce a heart attack?"

The brothers looked at each other and after swallowing hard, Merle answered.

"We got secret ways."

"Deal me in on them; we'll save a fortune in bullets."

The boys exchanged glances again, and after squirming under Johnny's gaze, Earl spoke in a whisper.

"He just died."

"What?"

"Matt, I guess we partied too hard and he died."

"You two partied with him?"

"He was a really nice guy, Mr. Rossetti, and he knew everythin' about college football," Merle said.

Johnny just stared at them for long seconds before getting up and pacing around the room.

"How many guys did you two whack before you killed Tanner?"

"None," Merle admitted.

"None? So what, Tanner was just a fluke?"

Earl shrugged. "Uh, heat of the moment, yeah."

Johnny laughed, but there was no humor in it.

"I'll be damned."

"Are you gonna hurt us?" Merle asked.

"Why would I do that? Burns is dead, that was the job and the job is done, but I think I'll find other work for you two. I should just kick you out of here, but for some damn reason I like you."

Earl smiled. "You mean we ain't gotta kill nobody else?"

"No, but expect a serious pay cut."

The boys stood and took turns pumping Johnny's hand.

"We don't like killin', but we ain't afraid of work. What do you want us to do?" Merle said.

"It's the weekend, so just chill and come back here on Monday. I'll think of something you can do."

"Is it all right if we hang around the bar for a while?"

"Sure, Merle."

"I'm Earl."

"If you say so."

The boys left the office and Johnny walked back behind the desk, shaking his head as he went.

"'We got secret ways,'" he says. "Christ, what happened to the third stooge?"

28

HE COULD ALWAYS EAT AT THE Y

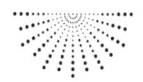

Sophia let out a sigh of satisfaction as she collapsed atop Tanner, her skin moist with exertion.

After a moment more, she slid over to his right side and laid an arm across his chest.

"If sex is all you wanted for helping me, I think we're even," Sophia said.

"I would say I've been overpaid."

"Seriously though, Romeo, I'll pay you for helping me."

"Keep your money, Johnny Rossetti already paid me."

"Liar, there's no way he paid you enough to compensate for all the crap you've been through since yesterday."

"I don't need more money; it was my pleasure to keep you safe."

Sophia kissed him, and her hands began exploring, but not with sexual intention, rather, it was an exploration of his previous wounds.

"You were shot in the chest once. That's a serious wound, I know, because my father was shot in the same spot when I was a little girl, and he almost died."

"Same here, I was down for weeks and didn't get my strength back for months."

"When was this? Where?"

"It doesn't matter."

"You don't like to talk about yourself, do you?"

Tanner almost said, "Which self?" but instead, he answered, "No."

"That's all right, be mysterious, I'll figure you out someday."

Her hands moved lower, and she found the knife wound he had received courtesy of Gino Tonti, in one of his recent battles against The Conglomerate.

"How did this happen? It looks fairly new."

"One of the ladies in my sewing circle stabbed me with her needle."

Sophia smiled and punched him in play. "Asshole, keep your secrets, and I just realized, I don't even know your last name."

"It's Montague."

Sophia laughed and punched him again, but harder. "Jerk! I'm not illiterate. I know that's Romeo's name in the Shakespeare play. I'm asking about you, baby. I want to know more about you."

Tanner rose from the bed and grabbed his boxers. "The less you know the better, and I think I've overstayed my welcome."

Sophia sat up, grabbed his wrist and pulled him back atop the bed.

"I didn't say you could leave."

Tanner ran a hand through her thick red hair. "I do have to leave soon… and I won't be coming back."

"Why? Never mind, you wouldn't tell me anyway, but when are you leaving?"

"I can stay until morning, but there's a bit of business I have to take care of tomorrow."

Sophia studied his face, then she gazed into his eyes as if she were hoping to find the things there that he wouldn't say.

"All right, so we have one more day together. But let's go out later. I want to go to dinner and see a movie, you know, normal stuff."

Tanner gazed downward and his hands followed. Sophia was still naked and her full firm breasts felt soft as silk.

Sophia smiled. "You are one horny bastard, do you know that?"

"We have to do something between now and dinner."

"Most people call that lunch."

Tanner pushed her to lay back atop the bed. "I have other appetites."

∼

Sara returned to her apartment building and found her sister waiting for her in the small lobby.

"Why are you here, Jenny?"

Jennifer greeted her with a hug. "I was worried about you, and since you wouldn't return my calls, I came to see you."

"Have you talked to Jake?"

"I did, he called me last night and said that you were drunk. Were you out all night?"

"I stayed with a friend," Sara said, and wondered for a moment if it was true. Was Johnny Rossetti a friend, or something more?

"Okay, I just wanted to see you and know that you were all right, and Sara, baby, I'm sorry if I hurt your feelings yesterday, but honey, I really am worried about you and so is Jake. I hope you know that we only did what we did out of concern and love."

Sara said nothing in return, and after a moment, Jennifer let loose a sigh.

"I love you, Sara."

"I love you too, Jenny, but please, don't interfere in my life. Yes, I have problems, but I'll work them out on my own, okay?"

Jennifer hugged her again. "I'm always available if you need me. You know that, don't you?"

"I do, and it goes both ways."

When they separated, Sara saw that her big sister's eyes were moist.

"We'll have dinner again soon, okay?" Jennifer said.

"Only if you leave the shrink out of it."

Jennifer smiled. "I promise, but I want us to stay close. I don't see you as much as I'd like."

Sara softened her demeanor and smiled. "We'll have dinner soon, I promise."

Another hug, a kiss on the cheek, and Jennifer was gone, leaving Sara with a feeling of loss.

Until she joined the FBI, she had told Jenny about everything that had been happening in her life.

Her big sister knew who had given Sara her first kiss, who she first loved and been loved by. She had kept no secrets to herself back then and a part of her ached to speak of the dark things to another person.

To tell them of her pain, of her sorrow, and disclose the desire for vengeance that ate away at her night and day.

But Jennifer would never understand such things, not on a gut level. She hadn't seen the parts of life that Sara had while acting as an agent and dealing with human scum, and she hadn't had anyone ripped away from her.

Talking to her sister or a psychiatrist wouldn't help, only action would, and if it took all the days of her life, she would get revenge for the death of Brian Ames.

Sara watched her sister climb into a cab and return to her normal life. She prayed that Jennifer would never know a tenth of the hatred that fueled her days.

Frank Richards, the new target was Frank Richards, and to aid in taking him down, she would search for Al Trent.

Sara took out her phone, placed a call, and heard it be answered after only ringing once.

"What's up, Sara?"

"Hi Duke, have you found Al Trent?"

"Not yet, but you know I will."

"Good, and let me know the moment you do."

Sara put her phone away while still thinking of Trent. He was either a dead end, or possibly the key to bringing Richards down.

She sighed. *Where are you, Trent?*

29
TICK! TICK! TICK!

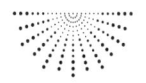

AL TRENT STOOD BEFORE A GNARLED TREE AND THOUGHT ABOUT the night Madison's mother died.

He had never meant for her to smash into the tree. He had been planning to kill Jenna Richards in her home and make it look like a robbery that had gone bad, but when he approached her townhouse that night, he saw her get in her car and drive away.

She ended up at a bar on Manhattan's West Side, where several men plied her with drinks, but she ultimately waved them all off, they weren't her type.

Jenna Richards liked her men young, and the younger the better.

Trent knew what her type was, he had heard the rumors among his peers and believed at least one of the stories to be fact, because he had seen her with the boy and when they noticed him coming toward them, he saw her pull one of her hands out of the boy's pants.

That boy had been Madison's boyfriend and prom date during her senior year in high school, yet someone else that Madison had chosen over him, despite his having asked to escort her to the prom first.

Madison had idolized her mother, and who could blame her, since her mother was the only parent that gave a damn about her. Frank Richards didn't have much time or concern for his wife or daughter, and Jenna Richards had tried to fill the lack of love her husband displayed by showering Madison with affection and praise.

Trent joined Jenna Richards that last night of her life and he could still recall the delighted smile she displayed at having run into someone she knew.

~

"AL, HI, IS MADISON HERE TOO? OH, BUT WHAT AM I SAYING, she'd never go out with you."

He stiffened at those words, while also realizing that she was drunk. She must have been drinking at home, gathering courage to go out and pick up a man.

"Mrs. Richards, why don't you let me take you home?"

"I don't want to go home, too many bad memories."

"But I thought you just moved in there a few months ago… when you and Mr. Richards began having difficulties."

"Difficulties? You might say that, the old fool can't get it up anymore without the help of a pill, and I'm still a young woman, aren't I? Don't you think I'm still young, Al?"

"You're very youthful, yes, but let's leave here. I know a much better place."

Jenna Richards narrowed her eyes and looked at Trent over her martini glass.

"I know what you're up to, Al."

Trent cleared his throat before speaking. "Wha… what? I mean, excuse me?"

Jenna leaned across the table.

"You want to be with me, admit it."

"Um, yes, I want to be alone with you."

"See, and if I was really old you wouldn't want me, so that proves it, forty isn't old."

Trent stood and offered his hand. "Let's go to your place."

But when they arrived there, they had to stop for a red light on the corner, and Trent caught sight of Madison entering her mother's building.

"Mrs. Richards?"

"Call me, Jenna."

"All right, Jenna, have you ever seen my father's cabin? It's quite nice."

"Your father died, Al."

"Yes, but the cabin is still there, and I have a key. Why don't we go there?"

Jenna opened a small bottle and popped two pills into her mouth.

"What was that?"

"They help me to feel good."

Trent shook his head. *Richards should have just let her be and she'd have likely overdosed or drank herself to death.*

He drove toward the cabin, which was on the outskirts of Tarrytown, New York, about thirty miles from the city.

He had only ever traveled there by one route, and after having to detour because of road construction, he became lost.

Jenna's car had a GPS navigation system, but Trent didn't know the address of the cabin offhand, only that it was at the end of a lane. He pulled to the side of the road and parked, to find a map on his phone, while hoping to see a familiar street name.

"Why are we stopping? I'm not getting in the back seat... unless you ask me nice."

Jenna was high and horny. Trent considered taking her for a moment, but then remembered that it would leave behind DNA.

When he couldn't get a signal, he stepped out of the car to see if a different location would help.

"Where are you going?"

"I'm looking for a signal."

Jenna giggled. "A smoke signal?"

Trent ignored her as he saw a bar appear on his phone, but then it disappeared. He went a few feet farther and was rewarded with two bars.

"Yes!"

The car started behind him. When he looked back, Jenna was waving goodbye and laughing hysterically.

"Come back!"

She sped up, and that's when the deer shot across the road. Jenna must have spotted it, because she swerved, left the road, and smashed the car into a gnarled tree.

Trent stood frozen in place for a moment before rushing to the car. When he reached it, he found Jenna pinned behind the steering wheel, and saw that a jagged piece of metal had pierced her abdomen.

She began to scream, as the shock of impact passed, and the pain began. The airbag had deployed, but it had apparently been punctured by the same piece of metal in Jenna's stomach.

She looked up at Trent with pleading eyes, as her voice escaped in a whisper.

"Help me, Al."

Trent looked down at the phone still clutched in his hand and saw three bars, then he looked in at Jenna and saw that she had passed out.

He stood there in the moonlight, listening to the drip of the vehicle's leaking fluids, as the radiator hissed, and the car, although smashed, still made that little ticking sound that modern cars make after you turn them off.

At the time, he thought that the sound was coming from the engine, but later learned that it was caused by the exhaust pipes, catalytic converter, and manifold cooling down. The metal made that ticking noise as it contracted.

Whatever caused it, to Trent, on that night, it was as if he were hearing the last seconds of Jenna's life ticking away.

Tick! Tick! Tick!

Precious seconds ticking away, seconds that became minutes, minutes that meant the difference between living and dying.

And for the rest of his life, when Trent heard that sound, he would think of that night.

Trent put his phone away, but then took it out and used it as a flashlight to check on the extent of Jenna's injury.

It was bad. Blood pooled on the seat between her legs and Trent knew that she would bleed to death without help.

He left her there, just walked away and made it back to the city by train.

Two days later, he was richly rewarded by Richards and became his assistant.

∼

Trent's phone vibrated and broke him from his memories. It was Gary.

"Get out of sight, there's a car coming."

Trent jogged a short distance to a stand of trees and made cover just as the sound of the vehicle's engine reached him.

It wasn't a car, but an old pickup truck. It must have been headed to one of the few homes that sat on the other side of the hill, where the road dead-ended.

Trent watched it go past, then he walked back to the van.

Gary pointed off to the west, where the sun was nearly obscured by clouds.

"It'll be sunset soon, are you sure that the girl will come here?" Gary asked.

"I can't be certain, no, but it's a safe bet."

"Or a waste of time," Gary said.

Trent ignored his pessimism, but he was beginning to doubt as well, because it had occurred to him that Madison could be someplace so far away as to make the sentimental visit arduous, and thus, unlikely.

He gave a slight shake of his head.

No. Madison was sentimental enough to make the trip, despite difficulty, and she would mourn her mother's loss, she would appear, he knew it. She had to, because if she didn't, he knew of no other way to find her and that would seal his fate.

Trent leaned back in his seat with a sigh and prayed that he was right.

30
LET'S MAKE A DEAL

Inside his Manhattan hospital room, Mario introduced his lawyer to the two FBI agents, Geary and Garner.

The lawyer's name was Kearns and he was a dapper little man with bushy gray eyebrows.

Geary was not pleased to see the lawyer.

"Does this man's presence mean that you've decided not to cooperate?"

"No, it means I'm not as dumb as you think I am."

"Meaning?"

"Meaning that I know I'm screwed no matter what I do, so I will cooperate, yeah, but under certain terms."

Geary's face reddened. "You don't set the terms between us, you two-bit hoodlum, I do, or I can leave you alone and go after your daughter instead."

Mario smiled at her. There wasn't a trace of warmth to it, but it was a smile, and it hid the intense hatred he felt toward her.

"Hear me out; I think you'll like it."

The lawyer, Kearns, spoke up. "I tried to dissuade my client from his course of action but was ignored. So I'm here to make sure that if we come to an agreement that it will be honored."

"I feel better knowing that a mob shyster doesn't like the deal," Geary said, and Kearns looked indignant.

"I am not a 'mob shyster' as you put it, Agent Geary. I'm a reputable lawyer with decades of experience."

"Whatever," Geary said, as she took a seat. "Let's hear the deal."

"It's simple," Mario said. "I'll show you where Lars Gruber and Tanner are buried, then you leave my daughter be and destroy any evidence against her."

Geary looked up at Garner, who was still standing. Dead or not, Lars Gruber was a prize and would raise their status within the Bureau. Tanner, while not the international fugitive that Gruber was, would also be a nice feather in their caps.

Geary looked back at Mario. "We're agreeable, but understand something, you can't just hand over these bodies and walk away. You still have to give us those above you, such as Johnny Rossetti. If you don't, we'll make sure that the right people know that you led us to the corpses. Once that happens, you'll be at the mercy of your so-called friends."

"I get that, all I care about is getting my daughter out from under the pile of shit you heaped on top of her."

"That happens as soon as we recover the bodies. How far away are they?"

"Not far, but not too close either. I'll tell you once we have a solid deal."

Geary made a face. "Please tell me that they're not in water. God, how I hate a corpse in water."

"They were covered in bleach, but they're in the ground," Mario said.

"We'll go tomorrow morning."

"That's good; the doctor told me I can leave then."

They spoke a little longer, mostly to Mario's lawyer, as they set about solidifying the terms of the deal. Afterwards, as they walked toward the elevator, Geary asked Garner what was wrong with him.

"What do you mean?"

"You hardly said a word in there, and if we return tomorrow with Gruber and Tanner, we'll have hit the jackpot."

"I just wish we had done it another way, other than using his daughter. The girl is an innocent."

"Fuck her innocence, she was a tool, and I'll use anybody to take these bastards down."

"Why is that?"

"It's simple. Johnny Rossetti is a media darling, anything to do with him will be front-page news. It's great publicity, an excellent way to get your name in front of the public."

They reached the elevator and Garner hit the call button.

"Now I see it, you want to get into politics."

"You're damn right, that's where the power and the money is. It wasn't all that long ago we had a mayor in this city who made his name going after the Mafia, and today he's spoken of as presidential material and worth tens of millions."

Garner laughed just as the doors opened and three people got off, leaving the elevator car empty for them to step onto.

"What was that laugh about?" Geary said.

"Nothing, it's just that someday I'd love to have a partner who simply wants to do the job and not be committed to some personal agenda."

"Everybody wants something, Jake, even you."

"That's where you're wrong. I've already had everything I wanted and lost it."

Geary shrugged. "Then you should go about trying to get it back."

"I can't."

"Why not?"

Garner stared at her and as he opened his mouth to speak again, the elevator chimed. After clearing his throat, he and Geary stepped from the car into a clutch of people waiting to get on.

"Jake, what were you going to say?"

"Forget it. I'll meet you at the office early and we'll get back here and collect Mr. Petrocelli."

"That's good, and come tomorrow, everyone in the Bureau will know my name."

Garner was looking forward to recovering Tanner's body as well. He hoped that once it was established that the man was truly dead, it would give Sara some measure of peace.

31
DASVIDANIYA

Vance settled into the chair in front of Johnny's desk at the strip club, then asked a question.

"How would you like to crash the leadership meeting tomorrow?"

"I thought that was just for Dons and Corporate honchos like Richards. Since my demotion, I don't qualify."

"True, but would you like to be there? If so, I can arrange it."

"Why?"

"That's easy; I liked what you put in that last envelope and want more."

"No, I mean what's the real reason?"

Vance furrowed his brow in confusion. "I don't get you."

Johnny slid a folder across the desk. "You're well-hidden enough that the cops came up empty, but we have federal connections too. What's your story, Robert Vance? Or should I use your real name, the one you were born with in Russia, Rurik Varanov."

Vance's calm demeanor slipped away as his eyes narrowed in anger.

When he opened the file, he saw that there was a brief

sketch of his life, including the fact that he had been in Russia's Federal Security Service, an organization formerly known as the KGB.

"I see Richards has underestimated you," Vance said.

"Hmm, now why would Richards have a former officer of the Federal Security Service at his side, one whose specialty was targeted killing?"

"Richards hates to lose. He had faith in Lars Gruber, but if the man failed, I was next in line for the job of eliminating Tanner. Unfortunately, Tanner died by other hands. I consider it a shame; I would have liked a chance to go up against Tanner. He was another man underestimated by Richards."

Vance stood. "I also underestimated you, Rossetti."

Johnny placed his hand atop the desk and showed Vance the gun he was holding.

"But you won't make that mistake again, will you, comrade?"

Vance laughed. "Rossetti, if I wanted to, I could take that gun away and force it up your ass."

Johnny cocked his head.

"That's interesting. You know, there's not a trace of an accent in your voice; still, the phrase should have been, 'shove it up your ass' not 'force it up your ass.'"

Vance's face reddened as he tensed up, and Johnny aimed the gun at his chest.

"I think we're done, comrade."

Vance stared at the gun, released a slow breath, then he walked to the door and left the office.

Johnny laid the gun atop the desk and smirked.

"Dasvidaniya."

32
CAN SHADOWS BLEED?

TANNER AND SOPHIA WALKED BACK TO HIS CAR AMONG A CROWD of their fellow moviegoers. Tanner let Sophia pick the movie and groaned internally when she chose a romantic comedy.

He liked Sophia, admired her grit and spirit, and if things were different, he might even stay with her longer.

But he had plans to infiltrate the meeting of The Conglomerate's ruling class and kill Frank Richards, and afterwards, he would disappear.

His hope was to kill the man without being seen and then Romeo would vanish. As Tanner, he was thought dead; as Romeo, he would disappear, and after that?

He had no idea, but would likely wind up somewhere else and start over.

"Did you like the movie?" Sophia asked, as she linked her arm through his.

"No comment, but I did like the company."

They reached the car and Tanner walked around to the passenger side to let Sophia in.

She put her arms around him and gazed into his eyes. "I wish you didn't have to leave tomorrow."

"It's best; we'd never last."

She pouted. "Why do you say that?"

"I can't stand romantic comedies."

He closed the door once she was in, then caught the scent of tobacco. Without being obvious about it, Tanner searched the parking lot. Past the moving forms of a family of five walking toward their car, he saw the glow of a cigarette shining from the rear seat of a jeep, along with the silhouettes of two men in front.

Tanner had seen that jeep before. It had followed them off the highway and into the movie theater parking lot when they arrived, but Tanner had thought nothing of it at the time.

The family of five climbed into their vehicle and the father started the engine and turned on his lights. When the brake lights illuminated as he put the car in gear, Tanner could see the ground beside the jeep, along with the five cigarette butts atop it.

Whoever was in the jeep had sat there waiting while he and Sophia were watching the movie.

When he climbed behind the wheel, he checked on the jeep via his rearview mirror and when he pulled out of his space, he saw that the jeep had moved as well. It was trailing behind them in the parking lot as they headed toward the exit and the Staten Island Expressway.

"Sophia, how certain are you that things have calmed down amongst your family?"

"We still have to settle on a new boss, but no one else wants me dead as far as I know, why?"

"There's a jeep behind us with at least three guys inside. They're following us."

Sophia slid down in her seat, turned and peeked one eye out past the side of her headrest.

"I see it and there are four of them, I got a look inside as they passed beneath the marquee. What should we do?"

"I'll make a series of right turns up ahead before we get on the expressway. If they go around in circles with us, we'll know they're serious."

"They'll also know that we're on to them."

"Yes, and it should force their hand. I'd rather face them now than wake to find them standing over us in your bedroom in the middle of the night, which was likely their plan."

"That's what we did with Adamo."

"Yeah and it would have worked just as well on us if they hadn't been sloppy. If the guy in the back seat wasn't a smoker, I probably wouldn't have noticed them and caught on."

Sophia shivered, then she reached into her purse and took out her gun.

"We're outnumbered," she whispered.

Tanner sighed. "As usual."

∼

Johnny, along with Joe Pullo, entered the nursing home where Sam Giacconi resided.

They had arranged for the late visit the day before and would use it to talk strategy about the next day's meeting of The Conglomerate's elite.

As the security guard opened the door for them, he told them that the facility's director would like to see them in his office.

When Johnny entered the office, he saw the lead doctor, along with the pharmaceutical executive who was responsible for the miracle drug that caused Sam Giacconi's recovery from Alzheimer's disease.

One look at the men's dour expressions told him there was bad news.

"Oh crap, what is it?"

∼

"They're not coming," Gary said, as he unwrapped the last of the sandwiches he had brought along for the stakeout.

Trent said nothing, but he knew that Gary was probably right. Madison wasn't coming.

"I was hoping she'd show too, really hoping, since Richards offered a bonus for… finding her, but let's face it. Nobody would come out here in the dark. You can't see a thing."

Trent looked out the side window of the van and caught a glimpse of the sky, past the branches of the tree they were parked beneath.

"The moon is nearly full."

"It's still dark as hell out here, and creepy. How much longer are we going to stay?"

Trent stared at Gary, who appeared to be just a shadow on the other side of the car.

"Creepy? Why do you say it's creepy?"

The shadow shrugged. "I don't like the outdoors, especially at night. Everything should be like Times Square, plenty of lights and people, even at night."

"I want to stay another hour."

"All right, but then we go."

Trent mumbled his agreement, even though he hated to leave.

He had wanted to see Madison again, to not only get answers and possibly clear his name, but he also wanted to see Madison, just to see Madison.

He had been infatuated with her since they were children, and, despite everything, he still wanted her.

Come on, Madison, please show. One more chance, that's all I want, just one more chance to make you see what we could be.

The shadow burped beside him in the dark, then spoke. "The girl's not coming, no way she'd come this late. All of this was just a stupid waste of time."

If Trent had been carrying a gun, he would have made the shadow bleed.

33
CROCODILE

The jeep stayed on their tail and once the men inside it realized they had been made, they decided to move in for the kill.

Tanner drove onto the Staten Island Expressway and sped up, only to see the jeep keeping pace.

Sophia was turned sideways in her seat, keeping watch on their pursuers. Tanner studied her and saw that her breathing had increased and that there was a sheen of perspiration covering her face, which glowed red in the taillights of the cars in front of them.

"We'll get out of this, Sophia."

She darted her eyes toward him, then stared. "You're so calm, why are you always so calm? Have you been in combat, fought in a war or something?"

"Why is your hair red? It's just something you were born with; steady nerves seem to be my gift. It's not something I've earned or developed."

"Nervous or not, this is bad, Romeo. We're outnumbered, and we don't even know what weapons they have."

"True, but none of that will matter in the end."

"Why not?"

"Because I'm going to kill them."

Tanner sped up, weaved recklessly through the thick Saturday night traffic and gained valuable distance when the jeep became stuck behind a slow big rig. Still, they were only a few dozen car lengths ahead, and the traffic in front of them was slowing.

Tanner pointed toward the line of trees running parallel with the highway.

"What's on the other side of those trees up ahead, do you know?"

Sophia took a moment to realize where she was.

"Yes, there's a small lake there, Lake something or other."

"Are there houses around it?"

"Yeah, but they're on the other side. Once you're past those trees, there's a slope that goes right to the water."

Tanner smiled. "Can you swim?"

"Sure, but what does that... oh hell."

Tanner saw a place on the side of the road where construction equipment was parked. It was just a gravel-paved area set atop the grass median, but there was room to park the car.

He flew into the small area going way too fast, but still managed to stop before slamming against the guardrail, as he sent gravel flying in all directions.

Before leaving the car, he popped the trunk to withdraw a bright orange breakdown kit. It once contained safety triangles and road flares, along with a cheap plastic hoodie. Tanner had turned it into a true emergency kit, and the box held a spare gun and ammo, among other things.

"They're coming!" Sophia said. She had already stepped over the guardrail and was near the side road that separated them from the trees.

The one-way road had traffic of its own and Sophia made it through a gap in traffic, but Tanner had to wait for three cars to pass before moving across to join her.

"Hurry!" Sophia called, and in an instant, Tanner was by her side, even as he heard the jeep skid to a stop behind his car.

Sophia ran well, despite the heels and tight skirt she wore, and they were at the trees when the sound of slamming car doors carried to them.

The slope past the first group of trees was steep, but there were smaller trees along the way. They held onto the trees and used them to keep from falling.

Most of the homes across the lake were lit up, but there seemed to be no one sitting out on their decks.

Tanner reached the water, turned, and backed into it as quietly as he could. He still carried the kit, and he opened it and sat it near the edge of the water, just left of his position.

"Get in slowly, but quickly," Tanner said, as he felt his feet sink into the mud of the bank and his clothes grew heavy from the weight of the water.

Sophia didn't whine about her shoes being ruined or worried about her hair, she simply followed Tanner's lead, while wincing from the shock of the cold water.

A deep, male voice cried out from the roadway in frustration.

"Fucking traffic, we can't get across."

Their pursuers were being delayed by the passing cars, but Tanner knew it wouldn't last long.

"Take a deep breath and hold it until you hear gunfire," he whispered to Sophia, whose eyes were wide from fear and the shock of the water.

Tanner watched Sophia submerge herself, saw the branches on the slope above them move, and lowered into the murky water like a crocodile lying in wait for prey.

34

WHAT ARE THE ODDS?

Johnny gazed with moist eyes at his mentor, Sam Giacconi, as he and Joe stood in the doorway of the elderly mob chieftain's room, watching him sleep.

The drug was a failure.

Sam, along with the other participants who were in the clinical trials, had shown remarkable improvement, but one by one, they had lapsed back to their former state.

The doctors had hidden this from Sam, fearing that the knowledge of his fellow sufferers' setbacks would depress him, or possibly even affect him adversely, by causing him to fear the worst.

They had been hopeful that he might be the exception and that the drug would work in his case, but that hope was dashed tonight.

Pullo turned and looked at Sam's doctor, an Indian man named Dr. Misra, who spoke with a British accent.

"So that's it... he's gone?"

Dr. Misra sent Pullo a subdued smile and shook his head.

"No, sir. If his condition deteriorates as the others have, he will seem like his old self quite often, particularly early in the day."

"You're saying that he'll be all right in the morning? How is that possible, he didn't recognize me or Johnny?"

"It's the drug, or perhaps the disease itself interacting with the drug. You may recall in the earliest stages of the disease that your friend suffered from what we call 'Sundown Syndrome,' where the patient experiences confusion and agitation at the end of the day."

Pullo nodded. "I do remember that, it was terrible, and then he'd be fine come morning. It was the symptom that made him go to the doctor in the first place."

"This is similar, only his deterioration will be much faster this time."

"How fast," asked Johnny.

"I'm sorry to say that he will be as he was before the treatment within weeks, possibly even days."

～

As they were walking back to Joe's Hummer, Johnny and he talked about the upcoming meeting.

Pullo sighed. "I know that Sam planned to speak, but he can't go now. If he had a relapse, or became confused, it would only help Richards."

"I know, so I'll go in Sam's place, or do you want to do it? Officially, you are the new Don."

Pullo pointed back at the nursing home. "Sam is Don, and after that, you're the Underboss, but I'll stand by your side as you speak, just as I would have stood near Sam."

"Thanks, but the words would have carried so much more weight coming from Sam."

They reached the vehicle. Instead of getting in, they both leaned across the hood and talked.

Pullo rubbed the back of his neck. "Damn disease, I know he's not young, but hell, it's a tough way to go."

"I'll meet you here before the meeting and we'll talk to Sam, hopefully we'll talk to him. If he's lucid, I'll explain the change in plans."

"Yeah, you do it; I'd probably choke on the words."

Johnny sighed. "Life is short, buddy."

Pullo waved a hand at him. "You're still young but look at me; I'm not a kid anymore."

They climbed in and Pullo started the engine.

"You ever think of getting married, Johnny?"

"Sometimes."

"I heard Sophia Verona stopped by the other day. Are you two starting up again?"

"No, she needed help handling Saul Adamo and I sent a guy to watch out for her."

"Who did you send, not one of those hillbilly brothers, I hope?"

Johnny laughed. "No, I sent Romeo, and the word is he and Sophia planted Adamo for killing Jackie and Vic Conti."

"Romeo took out Adamo? The dude sounds like serious talent. Maybe we should build a crew around him."

"We can't, he likes to go solo and he's heading back to California soon."

"He sounds interesting; I hope to meet him before he leaves."

"Yeah, I've a feeling that you two would get along."

∼

Trent was deep in thought planning his next move when Gary announced that there were headlights approaching.

"That's Madison, it's got to be."

"We'll see," Gary said, but there was a note of hope in his voice, because if it was Madison, he would be closing in on doubling his salary.

The car slowed as it approached their position, and when it

drove by them going even slower, they could see two silhouettes through the car's side window.

When it was ten yards from the tree, the car slowed to a walking pace, came to a stop in line with the tree, then turned the car's front wheels toward it, as if to illuminate it.

Trent grabbed the binoculars off the dashboard and cursed at himself for not thinking to buy a pair that had night vision capability, but when the passenger door opened, and a woman stepped out into the moonlight, he knew right away that he was looking at Madison.

"We got them."

"What about the guy, is that Tim whatshisname?"

Trent forced himself to move the binoculars away from Madison and place them on the face of the man who had his arm around her shoulders.

"It's him," Trent said, and there was disgust in his voice because there was no longer any doubt in Trent's mind that Tim Jackson was Madison's lover.

"She's got flowers," Gary said.

They watched as Madison laid a bouquet of flowers at the base of the tree, while Tim stood behind her giving emotional support.

"We'll follow them and find out where they've been hiding, and with you to threaten him, I'm going to have a nice long talk with Mr. Jackson."

"Sure, but hey, how old was the girl's mother? I heard she was real young when Richards married her."

"He married her when she was still in her teens, but she had just turned forty when she died."

"Wait, are you saying she died on her birthday?"

"That's right."

"Shit, no wonder the kid made the trip, even this late; it's like a double anniversary. What are the odds, huh? They've got to be astronomical."

"The odds are 365 to 1," Trent said.

"What? No, it's got to be more than that."

"Actually, you're right; the correct odds are 365¼ to 1, because you have to also account for leap years."

"That's it?"

"That's it. Dying on the same day you were born are long odds, but hardly astronomical. Also, many suicides occur on anniversaries, birthdays included, so I suspect the odds are lower still."

"I always heard you were smart, Trent, plus you called it on Richards' girl showing up here."

"That last part didn't take intelligence; I simply know her well."

"Were you two ever close?"

"Not as close as I'd have liked," Trent said.

At the tree, Madison fell into Tim's arms and he stroked her hair and kissed her gently.

"It looks like Timmy boy there has gotten pretty close to her though, hmm?"

"Very observant," Trent hissed, as a murderous rage simmered inside him.

35
MONEY!

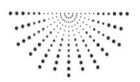

Jack Landstrom thought it was ironic.

He had cancelled a date to see a movie with his girlfriend, only to take a job where he wound up spending hours sitting in a movie theater parking lot.

There were three other men with him. Two of which he had worked with before and another man named Kalen.

The two men Jack had worked with were named Red and Silver. Red was called Red because everyone thought he was Russian. He was really half-Polish and half-Lithuanian, and whatever he was, his real name was too damn hard to pronounce, so he was just called Red.

Silver was easy to figure. The guy had a mane of silver hair and a beard to match. Jack liked working with them because they didn't give him any shit and always let him run things.

However, Kalen bothered Jack, because Kalen seemed jumpy, and he was young, not that young is bad necessarily, but seasoned is better. Plus, the dude smoked, which made Jack want to smoke again, and he hadn't had a cigarette since quitting a month earlier.

But what the hell, Kalen was Silver's friend and the job should be a piece of cake.

He had watched the man with the spiked blond hair walk back to his car with the hot redhead, and he was unimpressed.

The dude was... normal, just a normal-looking guy, and the contact had said he was a hard case. Jack had expected to see a guy like himself, six-five, two-twenty, and all of it muscle. This Romeo might be good with a gun, but they were four and he was one, and if things got physical, he wouldn't stand a chance.

Then Jack realized that Romeo had spotted them and became pissed.

The plan had been to follow them back to the house and wait until they were deep asleep. Then, they would enter the house, waste them, and bury the bodies.

That would have been good, nice and easy. Plus, Jack had planned to let his men have fun with the redhead before they killed her, like a bonus.

As he gave chase, Jack had been thinking, *What the hell, we'll just waste them out here on the road and go home early.*

They each carried an AR-15 with a full magazine of thirty cartridges. The new plan was to force Romeo and the girl off the road, then they would light them up and haul ass away.

The jeep was stolen and wore plates taken off another vehicle, so as soon as they did the hit, they would dump it and steal another car, along with another set of plates. Afterwards, they would drive back to the meeting point and wait for the rest of their money to be paid.

However, after Romeo made a suicidal lane change, Jack found himself falling behind. Afterward, a truck moved into the lane he was about to use to pass, and he had to sit and watch his target's car put distance between them. Jack feared that they might lose them.

That's when Romeo did a dumb thing. He skidded his vehicle to a stop off the side of the road, and he and the girl made a run toward a group of trees, hoping to get away.

Not a wise move.

There was a lake there or something, and there weren't enough trees to get lost in.

"We got 'em now!" Jack told his crew, and after parking, they went in pursuit on foot, the rifles held close, but ready, beneath their jackets.

∼

"Does anybody see them?" Jack asked, as he slid down the slope.

"No," Silver said. "But what's that on the ground over there?"

They had all spotted it at the same time; you couldn't miss it. The thing was bright orange and seemed to glow beneath the moonlight. But it was Kalen who first saw what was inside.

"Shit. Look! There's money."

Jack had time later to recall how stupid he'd been, not much time, but enough to curse himself.

Two thick bundles of cash were sitting inside the open box. The sight of the money made not only Jack, but also Red and Silver gather beside Kalen.

They weren't completely foolish about it though, they did swivel their heads about to see where their prey had run to. There was no one around, but the money caught their eyes, made them group together, and sealed their fates.

∼

Tanner exploded from the murky lake, and before his eyes had even cleared of the water running down his face, he sent a burst of gunfire to the spot where he'd left the box.

One man fell with two fatal wounds to his side. It was a guy with silver hair, and his gun bounced and landed in the water. Tanner had hit two of the other men in the leg, as his first shots had been low. They both stayed standing and took a bead on him.

Before they could shoot, Sophia came up gasping and firing. Her initial shots were high, but one of them clipped the largest of the men just above the left ear, writing a red line across the side of his head. He and the other men ducked while firing wildly.

That's when Tanner fired a shot that struck the young guy in the crown of his head, as the fool bent over to try to grab the money from the box.

The man collapsed backwards into another man, one who looked foreign, and knocked him back against the trunk of a small tree. As that was happening, Sophia had shot the big man in his gun arm twice, which caused him to drop his weapon and scream.

Tanner changed magazines and rushed toward the man pinned beneath the young guy, but he slipped when he was halfway there, due to the mud coating the bottom of his shoes.

The stumble saved him from being wounded. The trapped man managed to keep his gun and he had fired off two shots where Tanner had been.

Tanner returned fire and wounded the man in the side. That made the man arch his back from the pain, which shifted the corpse that lay atop him. It sent what was left of the young man's brains leaking into his open mouth.

The foreign-looking man sputtered, spit, and dropped the gun, so that he could use both hands to clear away the gore. While he was doing that, he cursed in a language that Tanner recognized as Polish.

Tanner stood above him with his gun pointed at the man's face, as Sophia held her gun on the big man. Meanwhile, across the lake, people were coming out onto their decks to see what was going on.

Tanner spoke to the man in Polish and asked him who sent them.

"Kto wysłał do nas zabić?"

Sophia did a double take at Tanner, but kept her gun aimed at the big man, who was lying on the ground and bleeding from his scalp and arm wounds.

The foreign-looking man stared up at him, surprise mixing with pain on his features.

"I speak English too, asshole."

"Then answer the question."

"Fuck you!"

Tanner kicked the corpse aside and fired a shot into the man's heart. He then moved over to the big man and asked the same question, this time in English.

"Who sent you to kill us?"

"The Conglomerate, but I don't know any names. It's all handled online, and I'm sorry, dude, really, just let me go, please? I told you what you wanted to know."

Sophia answered the man by shooting him in the chest twice.

The big man let out a moan, murmured something that sounded like, "Stupid," and died.

Tanner scooped up the box with the money in it and he and Sophia reentered the trees and disappeared.

36
NEVER SEE IT COMING

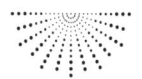

Gary pulled the van over to the side of the road, as he and Trent watched Tim's vehicle wind along the gravel driveway that led to the farmhouse.

"Shit, that was a hike," Gary said. "And I was hoping that we would follow them back to the city."

They could no longer see the car after it made the first turn along the driveway but knew that there must be a house beyond the trees.

"We'll give them time to settle in and fall asleep, then we'll go in on foot and break into the house."

Gary shook his head. "I'm not creeping around out in the sticks in the dark. Plus, we have no idea how many people are inside the house. Suppose they're not alone?"

"What do you want to do, wait out here all night?"

"Screw that, we passed a motel two miles back. I say we go there, get some sleep and be back here right after the sun comes up."

Trent gazed out at the driveway leading to the farmhouse. He was so close to seeing Madison again and clearing his name, but Gary's words did make sense.

"What if they leave in the middle of the night?"

"Let them. We now know what they drive and where they live. Besides, why would they run? They think they're safe here."

"All right, but I want to be back here at first light."

"Sounds good, but I also want to stop somewhere and grab breakfast before we come back. I'm tired of eating crap. I want some real food."

"If I'm not mistaken, there was a diner near the motel and you're not alone in wanting a hot meal."

Gary started the engine and looked over at Trent. All things considered, he liked the kid, and decided that when the time came, he would kill him in such a way so that he'd never see it coming.

~

AFTER DROPPING JOHNNY OFF, JOE PULLO DROVE AROUND FOR A while, but when he stopped moving, he found himself parked in front of Laurel Ivy's townhouse.

There was a light on upstairs, so he knew she was still awake.

Pullo, like Tanner, had never shied away from violence and had nerves of iron when involved in a firefight. The same could not be said when it came to affairs of the heart, and he feared being rejected.

He hadn't been thinking of getting close to Laurel, of dating her, not in the beginning. He had only sought to comfort her over losing Tanner, a pain he too suffered from, and one that surprised him.

He had always liked Tanner, but the loss was like the loss of a brother, and the shared grief had bonded him and Laurel together as friends.

His growing feelings for Laurel left him equally surprised and although she seemed affectionate toward him at times, he never wanted her to think that his attempts at offering solace for her loss had been a sneaky way to move in on her.

After sitting in the Hummer for ten minutes, he walked up the concrete steps and rang her bell.

By the time she came to the door, his palms were sweaty.

"Joe, hi, is something wrong?"

Pullo felt like an idiot, because it just occurred to him that she might not be alone. Laurel was young, beautiful, and smart, a Harvard-trained doctor for God's sake, she must have men lining up.

He held up a hand and sighed. "This was a bad idea; I didn't realize how late it was."

Laurel stepped out on the small brick porch in her robe and slippers and took a good look at Pullo.

"Something is wrong, what is it?"

"It… it has to do with Sam, Sam Giacconi."

"Oh God, he hasn't died, has he?"

"In a way," Pullo said, and as he said it, he could feel his eyes moisten.

Laurel took him by the hand. "Come inside."

"You sure? It's late."

"I'm sure, Joe."

Pullo let her lead him inside, and when she turned to face him after closing the door, he kissed her.

∽

BLOCKS AWAY, SARA OPENED HER APARTMENT DOOR TO FIND JAKE Garner smiling at her.

"Hi, I hope it's not too late, but I really wanted to talk."

Garner caught movement behind Sara and saw Johnny Rossetti sitting on a sofa with a bottle of wine and two glasses on the table in front of him. Johnny recognized Garner and smiled, as he raised his glass in a toast.

"Mr. Fed, it's nice to see you again."

Garner glared at Johnny before looking back at Sara with dismay lighting his face.

"Rossetti? Sara, you can't be serious. You know what he is."

"Yes, I do, and I've also begun to know who he is as well, and who he is, is a man who doesn't look at me as if I were mentally incompetent."

"I never said you weren't sane, but I do think you need help."

Sara smirked. "Johnny will be taking care of my needs tonight."

Garner shook his head in disgust.

"You just keep falling down, and when someone offers a hand up, you slap it away, but know this, I'll still be there if you need a friend."

"Goodnight, Jake."

Garner watched the door close in his face and, with a great sigh, he turned and headed toward the elevator.

When the door reopened, he spun around with hope.

"One more thing," Sara said. "Stay away from my sister."

And then the door slammed.

Garner stared at it for several seconds before he turned and left the building, with a heart that was as confused as it was broken.

37
MYSTERY MAN

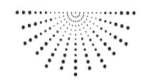

Tanner stepped out of the shower and found Sophia staring at him from the doorway.

After leaving the dead men on the shore of the lake, Tanner returned to the car and grabbed his phone, which he had left behind. With his belongings removed, he checked out the jeep the hit team had been using. It had been left running and the only personal items inside were a pack of cigarettes and a lighter.

He grabbed the lighter as Sophia pleaded with him to leave before the cops showed. She was drenched from the lake, as was Tanner, but Sophia was also barefoot, as her shoes had been claimed by the mud at the lake's bottom.

Tanner knew that the people across the lake must have reported the gunfire. What he didn't know was if his vehicle's license plate had been recorded by a traffic camera. He handed Sophia his "Emergency Kit" and told her to climb into the jeep.

Afterwards, he grabbed a gallon container of gasoline from his trunk and splashed the fuel inside and outside the car, which was registered under the fake ID he was currently using.

After activating the lighter, he locked the flame on high and tossed it onto the floorboards in front, causing the gas to ignite and fuel a fire that would erase all traces of fingerprints and DNA samples.

Ten seconds later, the jeep was back in traffic and headed for the nearest exit. After dropping Sophia at home, Tanner dumped the jeep a mile away from her house, wiped it down, and left it sitting unlocked and with the keys still in the ignition. Fifteen minutes after that, he was back at the house and peeling off his soggy clothes.

"What's up?" Tanner said.

"Who are you?"

"Are you asking me what my last name is again?"

"No, because that would be as phony as the first name, almost as phony as those tattoos."

Tanner had been watching Sophia as he dried off, but when he looked down at his arms, he saw that some of the temporary tattoos had begun to fade or smear. Apparently, the word "temporary" was meant to be taken seriously.

He finished drying himself by rubbing the towel over his hair and grabbed the clean pair of boxers that he brought into the bathroom with him. After putting them on, he gave Sophia a tight smile.

"I guess I've overstayed my welcome."

She went to him and placed her hands atop his bare chest while gazing up into his eyes.

"I don't want you to leave; I just want a few answers, a, a freaking name. Is that too much to ask, that I know the name of the man I'm—"

She sighed, realizing how close she'd come to saying too much, and very likely, the exact wrong thing. When she spoke again, her voice was less pleading.

"You saved my life and I don't even know who you are, can you at least tell me that?"

"I could, but if I did, it would open up too many questions, and Sophia, there's really no need to keep going on about this, is there?"

"I don't understand what you mean?"

"I'm leaving the city tomorrow. I told you that, I never hid that, so just think of me as Romeo and let things be."

"That car you torched, was it stolen?"

"No, it was legit, but was under a fake ID."

"And you speak another language, what was that?"

"It was Polish."

Sophia narrowed her eyes and spoke to him in Italian.

"Si può capire quello che sto dicendo in questo momento?"

"Yes. I can understand what you're saying."

Sophia gasped.

"How many languages can you speak?"

Tanner slid by her and back to the bedroom where he began to dress.

"What? You're leaving because I asked you to tell me your name?"

"Like I said, I've overstayed my welcome."

Sophia took him by the hand and gazed into his eyes, as her own eyes searched for something that wasn't there.

"You're really just going to walk out and leave things like this, aren't you?"

She saw it then, not what she wanted to see, but a faint reflection of it.

Tanner kissed her, then he gave her hand a squeeze.

"My leaving is the best thing I could do for you. If I stayed past tomorrow, things would go to hell fast, trust me."

"I do trust you, don't doubt that, but I don't understand you one damn bit."

Tanner let her hand go and gathered what little he had.

"I have to go now."

"I… at least let me drive you someplace."

"I'll be fine."

He left the bedroom and walked down the stairs with Sophia following. At the front door, she gazed at him with exasperation showing on her face.

"Whoever you are, you're a bastard, do you know that?"

"It has been pointed out to me from time to time."

Sophia hugged him and gave him a long, soulful kiss.

When it ended, Tanner opened the door.

"Goodbye, Sophia."

"You're welcome here anytime, mystery man, but be careful out there and watch your back. Remember, Frank Richards wants us both dead."

"That won't be a problem soon."

"Why not?"

"Because I'm going to kill him tomorrow."

Tanner gave Sophia one last look, then he walked out into the night without so much as a backward glance.

38
SECURITY BY TANNER

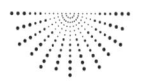

SUNDAY 7:34 A.M.

AL TRENT WAS STARING AT GARY.

They were sitting on opposite sides of a booth in a diner that was two miles away from Tim's farm, which the locals called Forgotten Farm.

The diner was nearly empty but would fill shortly with those seeking sustenance for the body before seeking it for the soul, in the church down the block.

Besides Trent and Gary, there were six other patrons in the diner. There were two couples, a trucker whose rig was parked across the street, and an old man who looked as if he had been hatched atop the stool he perched upon.

Trent and Gary had awakened to heavy rain and the forecast was for more to come, as a huge storm system approached from the Ohio Valley Region.

They also woke to discover that the van had a flat tire and found that the spare was missing. Fortunately, for them, there was a gas station across the road from the motel.

Gary limped the van over there and the two of them waited for the place to open.

Their plan to make an early assault on the farm had been pushed back and caused Trent to become nervous.

"Could you please finish your breakfast? This is already a later start than we had planned on."

"Relax Trent, they're not going anywhere. It's early on a Sunday morning and raining like hell out there."

"They could still leave."

"Maybe, but not for good. If we get there and they're gone, we'll just break in and wait and if they're there… we do what we do."

Trent pushed his glasses up farther on his nose before taking a sip of his coffee.

The diner they were in was quaint and old. It had been in operation since the 1940s and was a converted train car. Its exterior was covered in aluminum, which shined even in the rain, while inside, the chrome counter glowed in the glare of fluorescent lighting.

The linoleum tiled floor was worn down from the tread of endless feet, but the place was clean, smelled of good food, and the elderly waitress served it to you with a genuine smile.

"You do understand you're not to hurt them, especially Madison. Rough Jackson up all you want, but we do need him to transfer certain data to me."

Gary stared at him. "I know what to do. Richards gave me clear instructions."

"All right then, let's go."

~

BACK IN MANHATTAN, ON WALL STREET, TANNER WAS KEEPING watch on the overhead door that led to the loading dock of the building hosting The Conglomerate's meeting.

After leaving Sophia's home, he traveled back to Manhattan

by train and made his way to an underground parking garage, where he kept a stash of weapons, clothing, and a fake ID.

He had made worthless the phony ID he'd been using as Romeo when he had to set the car on fire. The IDs he used were of excellent quality and hadn't come cheaply from the source he previously used, but Tim had assured him that he would fill that need in the future, and for free.

His battle with The Conglomerate was a drain on resources, but he had hoped by proving his skill at killing, that in the future, he could raise his price and recoup any financial losses.

However, Tanner was dead, or so everyone believed, and he had begun to think that he should just stay dead, move on, and create another identity in another locale.

He had gambled against heavy odds that Tim would somehow break the encryption of The Conglomerate's files, and it seemed he lost that bet.

He didn't blame Tim for the failure, because the man had told him from the beginning that what he wanted was impossible. Still, he had hoped to do it and gain leverage over Richards and his ilk.

Richards had to die, he was just too damn dangerous to let live, even if he was Madison's father, and in time, Richards would come after not only Tim again, but also Romeo and Sophia.

~

Tanner had reached the underground parking garage after midnight and found the attendant asleep in the booth.

After easing by the man and avoiding the need to explain why he was there, he made his way to the rear of the facility, where he retrieved a hidden key behind a loose brick and used it to open the back doors of a gray panel van.

The windows were heavily tinted, while the windshield was covered with a cardboard sunshade, which blocked a view of the vehicle's interior. The sunshade was taped tightly to the front window and reinforced beneath by black plastic.

Tanner climbed in through the rear, closed and locked the doors, then put on a light.

The interior of the van held guns, ammo, clothing, medical supplies, equipment, and even food and water.

It was one of three such weapon and supply caches he had hidden about the city, and they were used to rearm and restock. In a pinch, he would also sleep in them, though not well, because of the restraints of space.

After choosing what he thought he would need to assault The Conglomerate's meeting, he climbed up front, settled into the driver's seat, and went to sleep, only to awaken four hours later when the two alarms he had set went off.

He exited the garage just after shift change and waved to the new attendant, who gazed back at him with a puzzled look.

Tanner was dressed as a security guard. He wore black slacks and black shoes, along with a white, long-sleeved dress shirt. Over the shirt was a black jacket with the word, SECURITY written in white on the back, and he had a matching cap to go with it.

There was a belt around his waist that held a radio, along with handcuffs and a collapsible baton.

Tanner had also coated his fingertips with a clear adhesive, so that while he engaged in the activities he had planned for the day, he would leave behind no prints, but only bodies.

He rode the subway to within blocks of Laurel Ivy's apartment and walked the rest of the way, with the intention of seeing her.

He was going to let her know he was alive and that by the end of the day he would be leaving New York City, and starting a new life elsewhere.

He had no expectations, other than that she would never reveal his secret to anyone. If she wanted to accompany him when he left, that would be fine, and if she chose to stay, so be it.

He was irked by the fact that he had never been able to erase her from his mind, even in the years they were apart.

Although he knew on some level that what he felt for her must be love, he was untrusting of the emotion because it made men fools, and although he knew himself to be many things, he did not list fool among them.

He spotted it from half a block away but wanted to make certain that it was the same one, and it was; it was Joe Pullo's black Hummer. It was parked outside Laurel's townhouse, covered in morning dew, indicating that it had sat there all night.

Tanner gazed at it for several seconds and then he walked away.

If Laurel and Pullo were together, then they were together, and he would remain a dead man.

∼

Tanner walked back to the subway and caught a train to the Wall Street area, where he continued on foot toward The Partners Building, where the meeting was to take place. Once he drew near, he looked for surveillance, but saw only the cameras, which were aimed at the building's entrances.

The street was virtually empty early on a Sunday morning, and Tanner settled outside the doorway of a brokerage firm, where he appeared as a guard standing watch.

And he was standing watch, but it was on the building across the street and two doors down, and when the limo appeared with a carload of bodyguards following it, he spotted it right away.

Frank Richards had arrived.

39

SHUT YOUR MOUTH

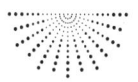

Johnny and Sara kissed once more as he stood in the doorway of her apartment, about to leave.

They had spent the night together, and he was the first man she had been with since losing Brian Ames.

As for Johnny, he'd had little more than one-night stands since the last time he was serious about a woman, which was over a year ago. The two of them wondered silently how serious the other was about their new relationship.

"Will I see you tonight?" Sara asked.

"If you'll have me, my head bouncer can run the club while I'm gone, or better yet, Joe Pullo."

"Pullo? He was in Brooklyn, wasn't he? At the sight of that pile of bodies Tanner left behind."

"Yeah, why, you don't like him?"

"I have little opinion; I will say that he didn't get rough with me like that animal that tried to rape me."

"Joe is a pro, unlike Vince."

"About Vince, is there a chance that I'll be running into him while I'm seeing you?"

"After what he did to you?"

Sara studied Johnny's face as she asked her next question.

"Did you have him killed?"

Johnny laughed. "No, there's no money in that. I put him to work in one of our chop shops dismantling cars for chump change, but I'll whack him if you want me to."

Sara shook her head. "If I wanted him dead, I'd do it myself."

Johnny grinned. "We are a pair, you and I, aren't we?"

"Are we?"

"I guess we'll find out."

They kissed once more before Johnny left to meet Pullo at the nursing home. Sara's building allowed each tenant two parking spaces in the basement parking area, and Johnny had left his car in Sara's second space.

He had just unlocked his car when he sensed movement from behind and turned to see Vance coming at him with a weapon held up in his right hand. A moment later, and the prongs of a stun gun bit into his right shoulder and he collapsed beside the car.

Within seconds, Vance had his wrists and ankles bound with zip ties and had gagged his mouth with duct tape.

Johnny attempted to struggle, but his muscles were affected by the charge of electricity and he was easily handled.

After opening a rear door, Vance dragged Johnny up atop the back seat with an ease that told Johnny that the man was stronger than he appeared to be.

Vance slapped him on the face. "Be a good boy, Rossetti, and relax, it will all be over in a few hours."

Then the door slammed, the car started, and Vance drove toward the meeting, where Richards waited to spring his trap in a bid to gain more power.

~

AFTER LOOKING FOR JOHNNY'S CAR IN THE NURSING HOME

parking lot and not seeing it, Joe Pullo tried calling him, but had to leave a voicemail.

Pullo walked toward Sam Giacconi's room, while dreading what he would find, and said a prayer that the old man would at least recognize him.

He nodded to the nurse, who was at her station and occupied with a phone call, then he pushed back the partially open door of Sam Giacconi's room and found the old mafia don looking alert, dressed in a suit, and sitting up in his wheelchair.

"Joey boy, what say we go kick some Conglomerate ass?"

Joe smiled, then laughed out loud.

The old man might be a candle in a windstorm, but his flame had yet to go out.

~

A CONVOY OF THREE BLACK SUVS WITH GOVERNMENT LICENSE plates sped along the Garden State Parkway on their way to exhume bodies and evidence.

Mario sat beside his lawyer in the lead vehicle, as FBI Agents Jake Garner and Michelle Geary sat up front, with Garner driving.

Geary turned in her seat and spoke to Mario. "You'd better not be fucking with us, Petrocelli, or I'll have your daughter inside a cell at Rikers by tonight."

Mario looked at her with a calm expression. "You'll get your bodies and then my daughter is free of everything, that's our deal and I'll keep it."

The lawyer, Kearns, spoke up.

"I don't like this deal and I advised my client against it. My dislike stems from the fact that there's nothing to stop you from involving my client's daughter a second time, and just so you know, Agent Geary, if and when my client is tried in a court of law, I will see to it that the judge knows how you comported yourself."

"Kearns?" Geary said.

"Yes?"

"Go fuck yourself."

Geary turned back around in her seat as Kearns sputtered in indignation. When she looked at Garner, she saw that he was lost in thought.

"Hey partner, what's up?"

Garner snapped out of his daydream and realized he didn't remember driving the last ten miles.

"I'm good, I just didn't sleep much."

"What was her name?"

"It wasn't that."

"Listen, if you ever need to talk, you know, give me a call. I'm not completely insensitive."

"Thanks, I'll remember, and the same goes for you."

They drove along in silence for nearly a mile before Geary spoke again.

"I uh, I looked into your past. Call it curiosity about a new partner."

Garner's grip on the steering wheel tightened.

"I don't want to talk about that."

"What happened, what you went through… it's a miracle you're still sane. I think if anything like that ever happened to me when I was young, it would have destroyed me."

"Michelle."

"Yes?"

"If you want to remain partners you'll never mention my past again. What took place happened a long time ago and I've moved on. Period. End of story."

"I can understand that and it's just a shame that—"

"Shut up!"

Geary looked at Garner and saw that his breathing had increased, and his face had reddened from anger.

"I'm sorry."

"Don't be, just drop it."

Kearns called out from the back seat. "Is there a problem?"

"No," Geary said.

"Would it be possible to stop for coffee?"

"Shut your mouth, Kearns," Geary said, and the caravan rolled on.

40
DEATH IS A CATERED AFFAIR

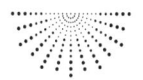

Minutes after Frank Richards' arrival, Tanner saw what he had been waiting for, as a white van approached from his right and headed for the entrance to the building.

The words, EXECUTIVE CATERING SERVICES were written across the side of the van in script, and Tanner could see three people sitting on a rear bench seat, all of whom were dressed in white.

He intercepted the van, looking very official, and with a smile of greeting. The driver slowed, put down his window, and looked at Tanner with a question in his eyes.

"Good morning," Tanner said. "I take it you're here to cater the meeting of Partners Inc.?"

Partners Inc. was The Conglomerate's cover name for the meeting, a fact Tanner had learned from the sheet of paper that Madison had reconstructed, after removing it from a shredder.

The driver smiled back at Tanner. He was blond with green eyes, very handsome, and Tanner thought that he was probably an actor waiting for his big break. The man looked like the rest of the people in the van. He was dressed in a white shirt with black slacks and shoes, was young, and willing to rise early on a

Sunday morning to make a living. His name was George, or at least that was written on his name tag,

George pointed across the street where the roll-up door was. "We go in there, right? I think I was here once before."

Tanner nodded. "Yes, sir, just pull up and hit the button. They'll either buzz you in or send someone down to meet you."

Tanner was hoping that they would just be buzzed in. If not, his entry into the building could be more difficult.

He made a point of looking at the trio in the back. "Why so few of you?"

"We were told to set up and leave, but there's a huge selection of food back there."

"It smells great. Well, you guys take care."

George thanked him and drove over to the door. A few seconds later, Tanner could hear him speak into the intercom and say the name of his company. Seconds after that, the door began to rise.

Tanner had been walking toward the opening with haste, but not looking rushed, and he reached it just as the van was about to drive in. He walked alongside the van as it rolled in and entered the gloomy interior of the loading dock, hoping that the van blocked his entrance from view of the camera.

George and his fellow workers noticed him, but paid him little attention, and Tanner entered a bathroom next to the receiving office, which sat dark and unoccupied.

He had been wearing Romeo's mirrored sunglasses and he took them off, removed the cap and jacket, and shoved the clothing inside the empty garbage can, along with the utility belt that held the radio and baton. The handcuffs, he placed in a side pocket.

He looked at himself in the mirror and saw what he wanted others to see, another one of the catering crew. The van he had slept in had several different outfits he could wear as role camouflage and along with the guard uniform, this was the look he had chosen to infiltrate the building and kill Richards.

The cuff of one shirtsleeve was tinged pink, but it wasn't obvious. It was caused by blood from a hit he had performed a year earlier, and the stain hadn't fully come out.

The black pants were a bit baggy, but he needed the extra room for the twin holsters he wore on his ankles. Inside each holster was a Ruger LC380, fully loaded and with a round in the chamber.

Tanner also carried a knife and spare magazines. He had kept the handcuffs in the unlikely event that he had to subdue someone without killing them, a situation he doubted he would face, but it paid to be prepared.

He opened the bathroom door and saw that the caterers had unloaded the food onto rolling carts with collapsible legs. They were headed for the concrete ramp, which sat on the opposite side of the dock from where the stairs were.

There was a man watching them and Tanner remembered seeing him once before. He had been with Richards in Las Vegas, along with another bodyguard named Gary, when he met with Richards inside a Walmart.

The man was big, but not a brute, and his dark hair was combed straight back, which was an unfortunate choice, because it tended to accentuate his nose, which was large and crooked.

Tanner didn't know his name and doubted the man would recognize him easily with the spiked blond hair after only seeing him once. It also helped that he was supposed to be dead. Still, he would try to avoid him, or else risk being discovered.

The last of the caterers made it up the ramp, and the bodyguard walked ahead of them as they entered a corridor that led to the service elevator.

After a minute, the sounds of their footfalls and rolling carts ceased, to be replaced by the squeak of the elevator doors opening, and that was followed by the sound of the carts bumping over the gap at the bottom of the elevator's threshold, and the closing of the doors.

That's when Tanner came out of the bathroom and headed for the corridor.

It was empty and appeared to have no cameras.

From what Tanner had seen of the food, it was all neatly displayed and stacked atop round serving trays. It was as the driver had said, they were simply dropping food off.

Richards wanted the building empty of anyone who wasn't a part of The Conglomerate, so that they could scheme in private.

Or was there a darker reason, one known only to Richards?

Tanner didn't care what the man had planned; he only cared about killing him.

He would kill Richards and then Romeo would cease to exist and join Tanner in death, as he moved on to a new identity and a new life.

However, death would be a part of that new life, or rather, the dispensing of it, because Tanner was a hit man, an assassin, a taker of lives, and would likely remain such until the day he died.

There was another corridor halfway down the first one and Tanner could see that it led to the building's lobby and reception area. After removing a gun from an ankle holster, Tanner strode down the corridor and went in search of his target.

41
US GOOMBAHS

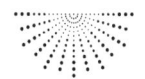

Trent and Gary trudged toward the farm as the rain increased in its intensity.

They wanted to take the couple by surprise, so they walked in from the road after parking the van behind a row of wild bushes.

Neither man had an umbrella or any kind of rain gear, so they were soaked by the time they were halfway to the house, which sat quite a way back from the road.

Gary cursed as he tripped over the end of a downed branch and nearly went sprawling atop the graveled driveway.

"Why the hell is the damn house so far from the road?"

"It doesn't matter," Trent said. "Let's just keep going and stay quiet; they're probably awake by now."

They reached the old farmhouse and saw that it appeared to be devoid of activity, and there seemed to be no lights burning within.

Gary gestured toward the rear, and they moved along through grass that was becoming soft from all the rain the ground was absorbing.

Gary peeked inside through the window set in the back door,

then turned his head and whispered to Trent. "It's dark in there; they must still be in bed."

Trent whispered back. "Can you get us inside?"

Gary smiled. "Piece of cake. Look at the lock, it's ancient, so is the wood around it."

Gary gripped the doorknob, pressed a shoulder against the door and pushed, but not with great force, rather, he slowly increased the pressure as he leaned more of his weight against it.

There was a cracking sound, which might have been loud on most days, but with the steady booming of thunder overhead, it just blended in.

That sound was followed by a popping noise, and Gary was pulled inside the house, while riding the door's momentum. He was just able to stop it from slamming back against the refrigerator.

Trent was about to follow him inside when he heard a sound behind him and turned to see the stray that Madison had taken to feeding. The mongrel was drenched from the rain and did not look happy to see them, as she bared her teeth and growled.

Trent took a step backwards into the house, and that's when the dog began barking in a strident pitch that not even the thunder could drown out.

Voices were heard, then there came the sound of someone stirring up on the second floor, followed by the sound of footsteps walking across floorboards.

"So much for sneaking up on them," Gary said. He took out his gun and fired at the dog.

～

TANNER WAS NEARING THE END OF THE CORRIDOR WHEN HE SAW a line of limousines pull up in front of the building and across the street.

It looked like the guests were arriving.

Tanner carried a set of lock picks. He used them to unlock an unused office and stepped inside just as both elevators chimed.

Opening the door just enough to see by, Tanner spied Frank Richards walking toward the entrance with five bodyguards. He then wondered how many more bodyguards were getting out of the limos. That question was answered by a booming voice, as a Chicago mobster named Sullivan Silva shouted his displeasure at Richards.

"This 'come alone' crap is bullshit, Richards. Do you know how many guys would like to put a bullet in my head?"

Silva entered the building and a beeping sound was heard as he passed through the metal detector near the door.

"Alone and unarmed," Richards said. "That was the agreement. Now please, hand over your weapon. I assure you it will be returned when you leave."

"Screw that!" Silva said.

An older man appeared behind Silva and placed a hand on his shoulder.

"Sully, we all knew the rules when we agreed to come here. Now, hand over the piece, or you can keep it and Jerry Mags back there can keep his too. You know how fast they say he is with a gun, and I'm sure that after all these years he's forgotten that you killed his little brother."

Silva looked over the old man's shoulder where a slim man with salt and pepper hair was staring back at him with undisguised hatred.

He took off his suit jacket, unstrapped his shoulder holster, and handed the weapon over to one of Richards' thugs. The thug thanked him and made him walk through the metal detector again.

Tanner watched them all enter and saw that only six had brought weapons. All of them were crime bosses and not the corporate types. The bodyguards took turns escorting the guests upstairs in the elevators, but Tanner saw that their number never dipped below three.

Three was a manageable number with the element of surprise in his favor, but he knew that the true criminal element among the guests would not be fazed and frightened by the sudden violence. They would pick up any weapon dropped by a fallen bodyguard and join the fray. He decided to bide his time and wait for better odds.

After delivering their charges, the limos departed and soon there was only one left. Tanner thought it odd that they weren't waiting around and wondered just how long the meeting was supposed to last.

When the black Hummer appeared, Tanner recognized it right away as Joe Pullo's. He also recognized the old man Pullo subsequently helped into a wheelchair. It was Sam Giacconi.

Shock registered on Richards' face and Tanner saw something else there as well, it was fear.

"Sam, my God, this is truly a surprise, as well as a great honor. It's so good to see you up and about again."

Tanner hadn't seen Sam Giacconi out in public in years, but knew the reason why, and wondered why Pullo would drag the old man to a meeting when he didn't even remember his own name.

However, the thought left his mind when Giacconi spoke in a voice that was husky with age, but also sounded strong and clear, by the vitality of its owner's spirit.

"Richards, you son of a bitch. Who the fuck told you that you could make decisions for my Family? I put Johnny Rossetti in charge and that boy is going to stay in charge. Nothing against Joe here, but this fucking Conglomerate shit has gone to your head if you think you're running things. We run things, Richards, us goombahs, and if you corporate shits need a reminder of that you'll get one, sure as shit you will."

Tanner smiled at the expression on Richards' face. He had

never seen the man look so flustered, and yet, you could tell by his body language that he was also enraged.

After taking a deep breath and releasing it slowly, Richards responded.

"I hear your concerns and… that's the purpose for this meeting, to air our complaints and grievances. Now please, let one of my men escort you up to the conference room and we'll get underway soon."

"Have you seen Johnny R.?" Giacconi asked.

"No, and he wasn't invited."

"I invited him, so expect him."

One of the bodyguards stepped on the elevator with Pullo and Giacconi, which left Richards with only two bodyguards at his side.

Tanner removed the other Ruger, and with a gun in each hand, he was about to charge out into the open when a man emerged from a corridor on the other side of the lobby.

It was Vance.

"Has there been any word back on the Verona woman and that man, Romeo?" Richards asked.

"Not yet, sir, but I'm confident that the team I chose was successful."

"Fine, and what about Johnny Rossetti?"

"Rossetti is secured."

"You didn't harm him, did you?"

"No, as you ordered."

Richards laughed like a man who had just received the perfect gift.

"Everyone and everything is in place, and as a bonus, that old fool Giacconi placed himself in the middle of it all."

"When will it happen?" Vance said.

"I'll let them prattle on for a while, eat, and get comfortable, and then…"

Vance bowed his head, as if acknowledging a master at work.

Tanner watched them all climb aboard an elevator; watched instead of killing, because he needed answers.

He shut the door of the empty office and leaned back against it.

What the hell is Richards up to?

42
THE FAINTEST OF SMILES

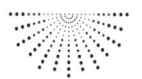

"Quick, out the window!"

"What's going on, Tim?" Madison said, as she stepped backwards out a window and onto a rope ladder.

The ladder had been installed years ago by the previous owners in case of fire, as a means of escape, and a means of escape is just what Tim and Madison needed.

"I don't know, baby, but that was a gunshot and I hear voices downstairs."

"Oh God, the rain is so cold. Tim, we need our jackets."

"There's no time, I hear them talking in the hall downstairs. Just climb, climb!"

Madison moved down the swaying ladder as Tim moved back into the room and pushed the dresser in front of the locked door.

On his way back to the window, he grabbed one of his sweatshirts, which was draped over a chair, then tossed it down to Madison, who had just made it to the bottom. It wasn't enough to shield her from the rain, but their jackets and hats were hanging near the front door and might as well be on Mars.

"Put that on. It's not much, but it's something."

Tim had just gotten into position to climb down, when he heard the footfalls on the stairs, and he was nearly at the bottom when he heard a crash. It was the dresser tipping over, after the bedroom door had been shoved open.

With time running out, Tim jumped the last eight feet. The ground was so sodden from the downpour that he felt his sneakers sink an inch into the grass.

Other than the sweatshirt he had tossed down for Madison to put on, Tim and Madison both wore jeans and T-shirts that they grabbed out of the hamper. The cold rain sent them both to shivering, or perhaps it was the sight of the two faces staring at them from the window.

Madison gasped. "It's Al Trent."

Tim didn't know Trent, but he knew the man's face from the newspaper accounts about the murders he was charged with. He also knew that the man worked for The Conglomerate and he assumed that the hood standing beside him did as well.

They had found him again, found him and sought to kill him, and this time, Tanner was nowhere in sight.

They rushed to the car, but then Tim realized that his car keys were still in the house, in a bowl by the front door. He had also left his phone behind on the nightstand. Living out in the country, while being on the run, he seldom used it and only kept it by the bed in case Tanner called during the night.

"We have to run out to the road and flag down a car," he told Madison, but as they took a step in that direction, a shot rang out.

They looked over at the house and saw Gary hanging at the top of the rope ladder and aiming his gun at them.

If they stayed out in the open, they would be killed, so Tim took Madison's hand and headed past the barn and into the shelter of the trees beyond it, as the two of them ran for their lives.

Mario stepped from the SUV and looked up toward the sun with his eyes closed, letting it warm his face. To the west, the sky looked as dark and ominous as inevitable death, but where Mario stood, the sun still shined, and life went on.

His peace was shattered a moment later, as Geary gave him a shove.

"Where do we dig, Petrocelli?"

Mario opened his eyes and looked around. They were in a clearing, surrounded by pine trees, and there were local cops and state police with them. They had been there waiting for them as their convoy of SUVs arrived.

They walked to the other side of the clearing and Mario gazed about, locked his eyes on a tree that had been split by lightning, and walked over to it. He paced off ten steps, looked down, but pointed back toward the tree.

"Dig there."

"There? Beneath that tree, you're certain?" Geary asked.

"Yes, dig there."

There were four cops from the town present. They walked to the tree and began digging, but before they had dug down three feet, Mario called for them to stop.

"What's wrong?" Garner asked.

Mario looked at him sheepishly. "I remember now, we buried them ten paces from the tree, not directly under it."

Geary got in his face. "What kind of bullshit are you trying to pull, Petrocelli?"

Mario shrugged. "I'm sorry, this is… stressful, and I got confused."

"You'd better not be messing with us."

"I'm sorry, Agent Geary, really, but I'm sure now, they're right over there."

Geary glared at Mario until she saw him squirm beneath her gaze, then she spoke to the cops.

"Dig over there now and if it's empty, don't worry. I know just who to toss into it."

Mario turned away from her. On his face was the faintest of smiles.

43
ABOUT THAT RAISE

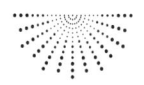

Joe Pullo was beaming with pride as he listened to Sam Giacconi make an impassioned plea to return things to the way they were, prior to the formation of The Conglomerate.

The aged Mafia Don was in good voice and his mind was cooperating, as he cited a list of recent instances of overstepping bounds perpetrated by corporate members of The Conglomerate, instances related to him by Johnny and Pullo.

Frank Richards sat across from the old man looking impassive, but a ruling member from the corporate side, a German named Heinz, stood and shouted objections.

Heinz was sixty, with a big barrel of a chest and a bald head. He was wearing an expensive pinstriped suit, but it fit his large frame poorly and the sleeves were too short.

"The old ways are dead, this I know, and in my younger years I too was a tough, a gangster, and I know the limitations of such a mind. You need us to run things, the world has become too complicated for savages. Let us lead while you follow orders. In the end, we'll all grow richer."

Heinz's less than tactful words created an uproar and the gathering became a game of let's see who can shout the loudest.

Richards stood, raised a hand and silenced the shouting enough to be heard.

"Calm down. This is why I called this meeting, so that we could air grievances and straighten things out. I suggest you all have a bite to eat while I go to my office and retrieve some documents that I left on the desk. If you require a restroom, there's one in the back, on the left."

Richards headed for the door with Vance on his heels, as some heeded his advice and walked to the pair of banquet tables that were set before the windows. They were piled high with pastry, breakfast fare, and urns of coffee.

However, most of the men continued to argue, and their voices drowned out the sound that was made when Richards shut the door. He had punched a code into the keypad to the right of it, and engaged the powerful locks, sealing the room and the fates of the men who were now trapped inside it.

With a shared smile, Richards and Vance walked off down the corridor and out of harm's way, as a cadre of bodyguards surrounded them.

~

MINUTES EARLIER, TANNER HAD STEPPED FROM THE ROOM AND back into the hallway. When he reached the lobby, he looked out through the glass front doors and saw the caterer's van drive away. He also noticed that the glass-enclosed security office was dark and unmanned and that the cameras were off. Richards and crew really wanted their privacy.

Tanner didn't know who Vance was, but he had heard him say that they had Johnny Rossetti secured.

Tanner assumed that meant that he was somewhere in the building. He headed for the stairs and took them two at a time, until he reached the top floor of the ten-story building.

Winded by the effort, he gave himself a few seconds to rest. He then entered a short corridor, which led to a longer one, where the elevators were. There were several doors running off it as well, and Tanner moved to the other end as quickly as he could without making noise. After dropping low, he moved his head until he could see with one eye what was around the corner.

It was another short corridor and it ended at a wall of glass with a door set into it. It was the conference room. Through the glass, Tanner could see Sam Giacconi speaking passionately about something, but despite being just twenty yards away, no sound reached him from beyond the glass.

Tanner nodded to himself as he came to the realization that the room was soundproof and that what he was looking at was more than mere glass.

He moved back the way he had come, and in the third room he searched, he found Johnny Rossetti bound to a pipe in the corner of the empty room. Johnny's mouth was gagged and his feet and hands cuffed with zip ties.

Tanner crouched down beside him and spoke in his best Romeo voice.

"If I had hired on with you, boss man, I'd be asking for one hell of a raise right about now."

Then he reached over and yanked off the gag.

∽

Tim tripped and fell as his left foot became mired in mud. When Madison bent down to help him up, she saw him wince in pain.

"Are you hurt?"

"I'll be fine, but try to stay on the grass; the ground is like taffy because of all the rain."

Madison shivered. "It's so cold. We have to find someplace to hide."

"We'll go to the office building. It has a roof and we can get out of the rain and make a plan."

Madison nodded in agreement, but then she froze as a form approached them from the bushes on their right.

It was the dog. Gary's shot had missed her, and the hound looked as frightened as Madison felt.

"Hi, honey, follow us and we'll get out of the rain and hide."

They headed for the unfinished office building and Madison saw that Tim was limping.

"You did get hurt. Oh baby, here, lean on me."

"No, I'll just slow you down."

Madison ignored him and helped him to limp along up the hill that led to the building site. Tim was not a big man, but Madison was petite, and soon she felt the effects of supporting his weight, and their pace slowed.

When they reached the building, they stepped atop the concrete floor with twin sighs of relief. After brushing aside pieces of discarded construction materials, they lowered themselves behind a square column set near the center of the building.

Madison wrung her hair out with both hands.

"This is better, but far from safe, we have to keep moving."

As if to prove her words correct, the dog growled, and it was followed by the sound of a grunt coming from the crest of the hill, as someone grew nearer.

Tim reached out and took Madison's face in his hands.

"You have to run. Head out to the road and get help."

"We'll both go."

"No, I would slow you down. Now go, there's not much time."

Madison spoke through tears. "I can't just leave you."

"I'll be fine. They can't see me behind this pillar and you'll be back soon with the cops. Now go, baby, please go."

They kissed, and Madison rose up, even as her tears flowed down her face.

"I'll be back. Just stay there and hide and I'll be back with the police."

Tim watched her disappear out the other side, with the dog following behind her. An instant later, he heard footsteps, as someone entered the building just yards away from where he and Madison had come in.

After looking around for anything he could use as a weapon, Tim stayed as still as he could. He hoped that whoever had entered would not walk where they could see him, but to his despair, the man approached his position on a straight line, while following the wet shoeprints that he and Madison had left behind.

Tim looked up, saw Gary glaring down at him, and noticed the gun hanging from his right hand.

"Where's the girl?"

He said nothing, and Gary grabbed his hair and yanked him to his feet.

The two men stared at each other, Tim, with his wet hair still gripped in Gary's fist, had his head tilted back to stare into the larger man's eyes.

Upon Gary's face was a rictus of pain and the gun slipped from a hand gone strangely numb, as Gary's other hand left Tim and was used to steady himself, as he leaned upon the pillar.

Tim backed away from him, his face showing a mixture of disgust and triumph over what he had done. Tim's right hand was slick with blood from the jagged piece of rebar he had shoved deep into Gary's gut.

Gary's eyes closed tight as the first wave of agony passed through him, but when he opened them again, he gazed at Tim with reproach, as if he should be ashamed of himself for fighting back.

"You little shit… you've fucking killed me."

Tim broke from his trance, picked up the gun, and hobbled off into the storm to save the woman he loved.

44

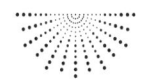

TRAPPED!

Mario sensed that Geary was staring at him, but he paid her no attention, as the cops continued to dig for the body of Lars Gruber, and what they believed to be Tanner's remains.

Kearns, Mario's lawyer, stepped in front of him and gave him a stern look.

"Are the bodies really here, or are you playing some sort of a game?"

"I'm making sure my daughter stays safe."

"That may be, but this does nothing for you. Once they unearth those bodies your daughter will be safe, but you'll be in a huge amount of trouble. They won't let you go, they won't ever let you go, Mario, and in the meantime, they'll constantly be asking for more. In my opinion, the best you can hope for is months of hell, followed by spending the rest of your life pretending to be somebody else."

Mario looked at Kearns with sad eyes. "I know everything you're telling me, looked at it upside down and backwards, and what I'm doing today seems the best thing."

Kearns placed a hand on his shoulder. "When the time comes, I'll insist that they place you somewhere nice. Just in case they try to use the Witness Protection Program as a last attempt at punishment. I won't let them send you to a slum. I'll see that you wind up on your feet."

Mario's lips curled in a smile. "Now that would be a good trick."

"I don't understand your meaning," Kearns said.

"I see an arm!" one of the policemen cried out, and all eyes turned toward the hole.

~

TANNER CUT JOHNNY'S ANKLE RESTRAINTS, AS JOHNNY UNTIED the rope that bound him to the pipe. After standing, Johnny slapped him on the shoulder and grinned.

"Romeo, I owe you buddy, but what's going on?"

Tanner explained quickly about the conference room and saw Johnny look concerned.

"Is Joe Pullo here? Oh wait. You don't know him, do you? But I have to get word to Joe."

Before they could say anything else, they heard footsteps, as Richards and his group approached.

Johnny held out a hand and Tanner handed him one of the Rugers.

They stood waiting for the door to open, but instead, the group settled outside the door and Richards gave Vance orders.

"The timer is set, and they'll have just enough time to realize that they're trapped before it activates, that will also give me the time I need to get clear of the building. When you're finished here, remember to call and give me a status update."

The knob on the door turned and Tanner crouched into a firing position beside Johnny.

"Would you like to have one last look at the patsy, sir?"

There was a pause, but then Richards spoke in a haughty tone.

"No. I had my last interaction with his kind when I left that conference room. From now on, I'll simply be issuing orders to them, and Vance, you'll be my conduit, with proper compensation, of course."

"Thank you, sir, I won't let you down."

"See that you don't. Now check the office I was using to ensure that nothing was left behind, then return to the conference room and make certain that there are no mishaps."

"I will and have a good trip."

There was the sound of footfalls that soon grew faint. Tanner held up three fingers, counted down, and ripped open the door.

Johnny followed on his heels out into the corridor and they found it to be empty.

"I'm going after Richards," Tanner whispered. "He tried to have Sophia and I killed last night."

Johnny gripped his arm as he tried to turn away.

"I want the bastard as much as you do, but I don't like what I just heard, all that talk about timers. That means something is about to happen in that room and my gut is telling me that it's a bomb."

Tanner's intense eyes went to Johnny's hand on his arm, but his anger turned to curiosity.

"What is that all over your hand?"

Johnny released him and stared down at his fingers.

"I forgot, but for some damn reason Vance sprinkled gunpowder over me."

Tanner stiffened, as something clicked in his mind.

"Not gunpowder, gunshot residue, it's not a bomb. They're going to shoot them and you're the one they picked to take the fall."

"We've got to get Joe out of that room."

"You probably can't, but Vance will know how to do it," Tanner said, as he moved toward the elevators.

"Romeo, forget Richards and stay here and help me."

"Go! Get Vance and I'll get Richards."

Tanner ran for the elevators, and after a grunt of frustration at "Romeo" not following his orders, Johnny went after Vance.

Johnny ran to the end of the corridor, saw no sign of Vance and approached the conference room.

∼

Madison made it to the road, but there were no cars in sight along the tree-lined avenue, so she began walking toward town. The dog followed along behind, looking miserable in the rain. Despite Madison's urging, she still would not come closer.

When Madison spotted a car in the distance, she ran toward it, and that's when Trent stepped from behind a tree and grabbed her.

Madison struggled as the dog barked furiously. She was a small woman, but Trent was no he-man. She broke free of him, but then he tripped her, and she smashed her head against the same tree he had hidden behind.

Trent looked at Madison moaning on the ground before he glanced about to see if anyone had witnessed their struggle. No one had, and the car that had been approaching made a left turn before reaching them.

Trent hit the yelping dog with a rock on its hindquarters and it ran off. Afterwards, he helped a dazed and bleeding Madison to her feet, and she shuffled along with his arm around her, much as she had helped Tim along just minutes earlier.

They reached the driveway of the farm, and when they were halfway to the house, Madison regained her senses, pushed Trent away, and staggered off back toward the road.

"If you run, I'll tell the man with me to chop off Jackson's fingers," Trent said.

Madison looked back at him. She was soaked to the skin from the downpour and her hair framed her face like a wet mop, but Trent still thought she was the most beautiful thing he'd ever seen.

"You're going to kill us anyway. Isn't that why you're here?" Madison said.

"Not at all, but your father wants the information that Jackson stole."

Madison hugged herself while shivering, as the cold rain continued to fall about them in torrents.

"I can't trust you."

"You don't have any choice. Run; go to the police. We'll be gone by the time you return. We'll be gone, and I'll see to it that the man I'm with tortures Jackson. Stay, and I'll make sure that Jackson remains unharmed."

Madison looked miserable as she thought things over. Trent was right, if she left to get help, they could take Tim and leave, and she'd never see him again, never know what happened to him.

With a heartbreaking sob, she walked back to the house at Trent's side, while praying that Tanner would appear to save them.

But she knew that Tanner wasn't coming, and that they would have to save themselves.

∼

JOHNNY PULLED ON THE CONFERENCE ROOM DOOR WITH ALL HIS strength and nothing happened. Inside, some of the attendees were still arguing, but a few had spotted him and pointed his way.

No sound escaped the room and it reminded Johnny of a silent movie.

There was movement on the right side of the room that caught Johnny's attention and he saw that a wall panel had slid aside. Behind it was an AR-15 rifle, like the ones Tanner had seen the bodyguards carrying.

However, this one was mounted on a swivel base, and instead of a magazine, there was a feed system attached that could supply six hundred rounds of ammo. It had been set to deliver three-round bursts, and the laser-targeting that controlled it would make certain that it hit what it was aimed at.

Panic emerged on many faces at the sight of the gun and one of the men walked toward it. He was one of The Conglomerate's corporate members and he was the first to die.

Blood spurted from the man and he toppled to the floor.

Johnny took a step away from the door at the silent scene of death, as the surrealistic quality of it startled him.

Another died, then another. One man dived beneath one of the tables where the food was set-up, and when a volley of shots perforated the coffee urns, the scalding liquid spilled over and burned his neck and back.

However, his agony was brief, because a few moments later, the gun swiveled his way once more as he jumped to his feet, and he was blasted with three shots to the chest.

That's when the mad rush for the door began. Several men reached it, tried in vain to open it and gazed at Johnny with eyes begging to be saved.

Johnny looked past the mob on the other side of the door and searched for Pullo and Sam. They were on the floor beneath the conference table and Pullo was shielding the old man with his body.

And at the door, the bodies began to fall, as the rifle fired without ceasing.

45

THE OLE SHOE TRICK

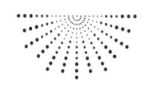

In the building's lobby, Frank Richards strode off the elevator surrounded by six armed bodyguards, while knowing that on the top floor, those who would oppose him were meeting their end.

He was so engrossed in thoughts of future glory, of gaining power, that he hadn't heard what one of the bodyguards had said.

"Sir?"

"What is it?"

The man pointed at the display above the other elevator. "Someone's coming down, but stopping on each floor, and I thought Mr. Vance was in your office."

Richards furrowed his brow as he watched the elevator display show that the other car was descending.

"Escort me to the limousine, then two of you will come back and deal with whoever it is."

They continued toward the front doors, but when they reached them, they saw that the handles of the doors were connected by a set of handcuffs, which only allowed them to open a few inches.

"What is going on?" Richards asked.

The bodyguards all gave him blank looks as the other elevator door chimed.

The men turned as one, as Richards hid behind them. When the doors on the elevator slid aside, all that could be seen was the tip of a black shoe.

"Whoever is in there, come out with your hands raised," the lead bodyguard said.

There was no answer, and with a move of his head, the man sent two of his men to check out the elevator.

~

Tanner reached the bottom of the stairs, cracked opened the door, and saw two of Richards' bodyguards going to check out the elevator he had left his shoes in.

The men all had their backs to him, with Richards at the rear, peeking over the shoulder of the guard Tanner had recognized from Las Vegas.

In his stocking feet, Tanner came up behind them, fired head shots at the two bodyguards near the elevator, and as the rest of the men spun around at the sound of gunfire, he grabbed the familiar guard by the knot of his tie, shoved his gun in the man's waistband and shot him in the groin, twice.

The man screamed, sagged, but Tanner held him up as the other bodyguards fired, and Richards cowered near the door.

Tanner let the dying guard drop to his knees, then used him as a shield. After dropping his Ruger, Tanner grabbed up the wounded man's rifle. It was set on semi-auto and Tanner aimed at the bodyguards' legs, on the assumption that they too were wearing vests, much like the one the man who shielded him wore.

Two of the remaining three guards went down screaming in pain from leg wounds, while the last one kept firing round after round. Tanner emptied his gun, but only managed to wound the man in his arm. Thinking that Tanner was out of ammo, the man grew bold and drew closer.

Tanner shoved the now dead guard at the man's feet, which caused him to dance to the side, and gave Tanner the time he needed to grab his Ruger from the floor. He shot the man twice in the head.

One of the wounded bodyguards fired at Tanner, but he was sitting up on the floor and his shots went high. Tanner hit the man with another shot to the leg and saw him drop his weapon and scream. He shot him again and the scream died.

The guards were all down, five dead, one wounded, as the other guard wounded in the leg lay on his back moaning loudly, his weapon just feet away, but forgotten.

Toward the end of the firefight, Richards had fled down the corridor that Tanner had been in earlier. He was probably hoping to reach the loading dock door and escape.

It was not to be, as Tanner sent one of his two remaining shots down the corridor and struck Richards in the back, which sent the man sprawling atop the polished marble floor.

Tanner grabbed a rifle from one of the bodyguards who had died first near the elevator, retrieved his shoes, and placed a mercy round into the surviving guard's forehead. With that done, he walked back past the front doors, which were secured with the handcuffs he had placed on them before going upstairs.

Following the trail of blood that Richards left behind, he saw that the man had tried to crawl away to safety, but there was no safety in Richards' future, only imminent death.

∽

Trent wiped away the water that was still dripping down from his hair, then he opened Tim's laptop.

"What's the password?" Trent asked, and when Madison wouldn't speak, he threatened once more to have Tim tortured, which caused her to give him the password.

"Stop fighting me, Madison. I'm not here to hurt you."

The laptop was the one that Tim had dedicated to breaking the encryption, so Trent had no difficulty finding what he was looking for. He paused for a moment, recalled the sequence and input the correct alphanumeric combination, which decoded the files.

"It all looks to be here, but I'll need every copy."

Madison stared at him with a curious gaze. "What happened to you, Al? When we were kids, you weren't like this. You were just a sweet nerdy boy who couldn't wait to grow up. What made you what you are now?"

"And just what do you think I am, Madison?"

"A murderer, the man who killed my mother."

"Your mother brought about her own end; I just chose not to intercede."

"You admit you were there when she died?"

"Yes, and despite the sainted image you have of her, your mother was drunk that night and high on something. She could have just as easily run me over as collide into that tree."

Realization dawned on Madison's face.

"That's how you found us, isn't it? You were watching the tree and saw me visit?"

"Yes, but why so late?"

"We had car trouble; a fan belt broke out on the highway."

"Ah," Trent said, before checking his watch; his new watch, as the old one had been sacrificed to find Madison. "Where is Gary? He must have caught Jackson by now."

He took out his phone, but then heard footsteps on the front porch.

"Here they are."

He pointed at Madison. "Stay put."

She glared at him in return and Trent went to the door, opened it, and found Tim pointing a gun at him.

"Madison!" Tim shouted.

She rushed to him, as relief flooded her features, but when

she came even with Trent, he shoved her toward Tim and ran into the living room, headed for the back door.

Tim and Madison had both taken shooting lessons from Tanner, but rarely hit what they were shooting at. Tanner had told them that it took time for most people to learn to shoot well, as he schooled them on firearms and the proper way to sight and hit a target.

None of what he had learned was in Tim's mind as he raised the gun and fired. Still, Trent stumbled and yelped, as the phone still clutched in his hand, went flying and he landed on the floor beside the sofa.

Before they could get to him, Trent rolled over, used the sofa to help rise to his feet, then ran into the hallway that led to the rear door.

When Madison helped Tim limp into the living room, they found blood on the floor near the sofa.

Madison grinned. "You got him."

46
HEY... WEREN'T YOU DEAD?

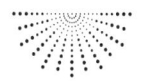

Tanner figured his shot had inflicted damage to Richards' spine and that the man could no longer walk. When he reached him, he turned him over onto his back with one hand and glared down at him.

Richards' face was a mask of pure terror, but then Tanner saw the glimmer of recognition form. Despite the spiked blond hair, Richards recognized him, and the terrorized expression morphed into one of confusion.

"Tanner?"

"Yes."

"You're... you're dead."

"I think that's my line," Tanner said, as he placed the rifle against Richards' forehead.

Realization dawned on Richards' face, coupled with a look of amazement.

He was Franklin Quentin Richards, the eldest son of Carlton Bane Richards and the grandson of Wall Street legend, Preston Harcourt Richards.

Men such as he did not die on their backs at the hands of a thug, they forged financial empires, influenced world markets, and ruled, above all else, they ruled. For Frank Richards, the concept of dying had always been abstract, never impending.

He was to have died a very old man inside the walls of his palatial estate, after having spent a lifetime accumulating power. And to die now, when he was so close to grabbing fistfuls of raw power, of becoming the sole directing force behind The Conglomerate, it was… inconceivable.

He stared up at Tanner and said four words with total conviction. "You can't do this!"

"Wanna bet?"

Tanner placed one round in Richards' head, followed by a shot to the heart.

With that done, he strode to a door marked, **ELECTRICAL**, and blew the lock apart. He then entered the small room, and with a snap of the main breaker, Tanner shut down the power to the building.

He had hesitated for just a second before hitting the switch. Not only because inaction could bring death to many, if not all of The Conglomerate's leadership, an organization that had vowed to kill him, but also because Joe Pullo was inside whatever trap Richards had set; Joe Pullo, who was now sleeping with Laurel Ivy.

But the same man who caused him to hesitate in taking the action was also the reason for its execution. Tanner did not wish Pullo dead and he would save him if he could.

With a sigh, he left the tiny room, stepped over Richards' corpse, and went to see if shutting off the power had made any difference in whatever was going on.

~

OUTSIDE THE CONFERENCE ROOM, JOHNNY STARED IN AT THE dormant gun, which had killed so many.

Most of The Conglomerate's corporate members were

dead. They had rushed toward the door in a blind panic and the gun picked them off with ease.

A few Mafioso were dead as well, but they were men who had come up on the streets, and generally knew when to take cover.

Pullo had moved Sam into a corner when it became apparent that the gun had been programmed to not only track movement, but to also deliver random shots about the room, including the conference table, whose wood surface provided little cover from a .223 Remington cartridge.

Seeing his chance, Pullo rushed toward the gun. He tried to free it from its swivel base without luck, but did managed to pull the feeder from the clip holder and extract the round in its chamber.

Upon seeing this, Johnny had breathed a sigh of relief, but then tensed up, as he heard someone approaching, because his gun was empty. In frustration, he had used every round to try to shatter the door without even scratching it.

It was Tanner, with his dyed blond hair looking orange beneath the red glow of the emergency lights. When Johnny saw him, he smiled.

"You cut the power, didn't you?"

"Yeah, did it work?"

"It did, but a lot of guys had already died."

"Richards is one of them."

Johnny grinned and punched him on the shoulder. "Good man, but what about Vance?"

Johnny got his answer, as Vance came around the corner with a rifle in his hand and opened fire.

47
HIDEY-HOLE

The bodies of Lars Gruber and Jackie Verona had been pulled from the ground and Mario had honored his agreement.

Geary was flying high and knew that with double murder charges hanging over his head, Mario would cooperate and wear a wire.

Hell, she'd be willing to bet he'd wear a tutu if she told him to put one on.

She looked over at Mario and saw that he was staring at her.

"Why so glum? Your daughter is safe, just like you wanted."

Mario walked off toward the trees. "I have to take a leak."

Geary watched him go, suspicious and worried that he might do something stupid like try to run off through the trees. What she didn't expect him to do, was to grab a shovel and start digging inside the first hole the cops had dug, the one he had said was a mistake.

Geary walked over, Garner too, along with Kearns the lawyer and a state trooper.

They watched him dig, and all four of them wore expressions that revealed fascination and confusion.

"Mario," Kearns said. "What are you doing?"

Mario removed three more piles of dirt, tossed the shovel aside, and sat on the edge of the hole, to gaze up at Geary.

"The body that was shot so many times, that was Tanner. He had been hiding inside a box, a portable toilet, then he jumped out and surprised Gruber. Would you like to see the box?"

Geary pointed at the hole. "Is it down there?"

"It is, along with Gruber's gun."

Mario had been reaching down into the hole as he spoke. When his hand emerged, it was holding a weapon.

The gun had been buried in the ground for nearly two weeks, but unfortunately for Geary, it still worked.

Mario aimed upwards at her startled face and the bullet caught her just above the lips and sent her tumbling backwards.

Garner caught her, as the state trooper fired three shots into Mario's torso, killing him.

Mario's lawyer, Kearns, was making a keening sound after witnessing the violence, and when he looked over at Geary and saw what a 9mm bullet did to a human skull upon exiting, he fell to his knees and vomited.

Garner was calling Geary's name, even though he knew she was dead. The one thought that kept going through his mind were words that Geary had said the night before.

Come tomorrow, everyone in the Bureau will know my name.

And they would, as news of the death of a fellow agent traveled fast.

Garner wiped away tears cried for a woman he hadn't even liked, as another partnership ended in gunfire.

48
SUCH SWEET SORROW

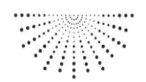

Trent was seeing double by the time he reached Gary's van, and if not for the heavy rain continually washing it away, he would have been a bloody mess.

Tim's shot had entered Trent's back, bounced off a rib and performed malicious acts on his intestines, before coming to rest inside his spleen.

Trent had never felt so much pain, but fear of death kept him on his feet and moving through the rain, despite the agony. He climbed inside the van and moaned in pleasure from the relief of it, that is, until he remembered that he didn't have the keys, Gary did.

"Here."

The soft voice came from behind and startled him so that he cried out.

It was Gary. He was stretched out on his back in the rear of the van with an ugly rusted piece of pipe jutting out of his stomach. The floor beneath him was stained red with blood.

"Here," Gary said again, and this time, Trent saw that he was holding up the keys to the van.

"What happened to you, Jackson?"

Gary nodded and closed his eyes.

Trent started the van, felt the mud cling to the tires as if to hold it in place, but then got it moving and back out onto the wet road. The wipers were going double-time and still Trent was having trouble seeing.

The problem didn't lie in the weather conditions alone, but also in the driver, as Trent's eyesight blurred.

He blamed it on his glasses, which were still spattered with rain, and he reached down to take a tissue from the center console.

He whipped the glasses off, wiped them dry, and placed them back on his face just in time to see the deer standing in the road.

Reflexively, he swerved to avoid the creature, jumped the curb and flipped the van.

As he lay inside the van waiting for someone to rescue him, Trent remembered the deer that Madison's mother had swerved to avoid and wondered if it had somehow been the same animal he had just seen.

It was the last thought he would ever have.

~

TANNER DROPPED TO THE FLOOR ALONG WITH JOHNNY, EVEN AS Vance opened up with the rifle. Johnny was armed with Tanner's other Ruger, but the gun was empty, so he lay sideways against the wall to try to make himself a smaller target.

Tanner fired back with his own rifle and Vance retreated after a bullet tore across his right cheek. Vance had been holding a bag in his other hand, but let it drop to the floor before running off.

Tanner rose to go in pursuit and Johnny joined him.

"I'm empty, Romeo."

Without slowing down, Tanner took a spare magazine from a side pocket and passed it to Johnny, who ejected the spent magazine and fed in the fresh one while keeping pace.

When they reached the spot where Vance had been, they saw the bag he'd dropped, along with its contents, which had spilled out atop the carpet. They were more spent magazines, the type used in an AR-15. Tanner assumed that Vance had been coming to the room to plant them as evidence.

When they reached the elevators, Johnny slowed, but then he remembered that the power was out and rushed with Tanner toward the stairs, which were at the other end of the short corridor facing them.

There was a door on either side of the hallway and Tanner wondered if Vance had hidden within one of the rooms. Then he spotted the tiny drops of blood whose trail disappeared behind the stairwell door.

Tanner opened the door with caution and heard Vance's footfalls come from below. He and Johnny followed Vance by practically leaping down the dimly lit stairs and heard the door at the bottom bang open and then close.

Johnny left the stairwell to stare in shocked surprise at the bodies of Richards' bodyguards, while a string of Russian curses came from the other end of the building, as Vance stumbled upon the body of Frank Richards.

Vance was just a dark shape in the gloom of the emergency lighting, but Johnny fired on him. However, the man had already moved on, and was headed toward the loading dock and the street beyond.

Tanner and Johnny gave chase, but when they went outside, they saw no sign of Vance.

The Russian had escaped.

When they returned inside, Tanner restored the power, after Johnny told him about Pullo disarming the swivel-mounted rifle.

"I still have to get them out of that room, any suggestions?"

"There was a keypad, wasn't there?"

"Yeah, why?"

Tanner recalled something that Tim had said, when he told him the story of breaking into Richards' computer.

"When you get upstairs, try typing in the word, MUMSY. I've a hunch it will work."

"All right, but what do you mean when I get upstairs, aren't you coming too?"

"I'm done, boss man, I did what I came here to do and now it's time I've left the city."

Johnny offered his hand, Tanner took it and the two men shook.

"At least come by the club later so I can pay you for what you've done, and I promise you, I'll be generous."

"You can repay me by looking out for Sophia Verona. Don't let anything happen to her."

"I'll do that. She means something to me too, it's why I sent you to watch over her in the first place, but I still owe you, Romeo. If there's ever anything you want, just ask."

"I'll do that," Tanner said.

After discarding the blood-spattered white shirt, under which he wore a black Tee, Tanner walked through the loading dock and out onto the street with a strange feeling of peace. He was believed to be dead and could move on and start over.

He had planned to catch a cab, but walked instead, when he realized that he might never return to the city. He liked Manhattan, liked the hustle and energy, and the anonymity the city could offer.

But not to him, he was burned in New York and would start fresh somewhere else. As someone else?

If so, it was not an experience he was unfamiliar with.

49
LEVERAGE

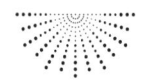

"It's all here, holy crap, it's all here!"

Tim's sprained ankle was forgotten as he studied his laptop screen. While checking the files, Trent had accessed them by entering the correct code and never got the chance to close it again.

Madison sat beside him on the sofa. "This means we're safe, doesn't it?"

"Yes, us and Tanner, we can hold these financial records over their heads and blackmail them. They wouldn't dare touch us, couldn't touch us, not without destroying themselves. If the IRS had these, it would be disastrous for The Conglomerate."

Tim sent copies of the decoded files to numerous cloud storage sites, printed out two hard copies, then closed the laptop. While he was doing that, Madison had cleaned up Trent's blood, secured the back door, and loaded a suitcase into the car.

They couldn't stay at the farm with Trent on the loose and had no way of knowing who else would come. Tim also needed to see a doctor about his ankle, while Madison had treated the scrape on her forehead and bandaged it.

When they drove off, they came upon a bad accident. The

sparse traffic was halted as they waited for the ambulance to remove the victims.

"That's a shame," Tim said. "Someone flipped that van; they must have been traveling too fast in this downpour."

Madison agreed, while also saying that she hoped there were no children inside.

In the coming days, they would learn who had been inside that van, and they would both smile at the knowledge.

50
A MATCHED SET

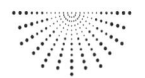

DAYS LATER

Inside Johnny R's strip club, the stage was quiet because the hour was early, but a meeting was taking place in Johnny's office.

Present were Johnny, Joe Pullo, and Sophia Verona.

Johnny had asked Sophia there to give her the sad news.

"It was my father, not Tanner?"

Johnny nodded solemnly. "Yeah honey, Jackie must have been out to kill Gruber as payback for killing your brother, and he got some too… but died for it."

Pullo shook his head. "Tanner was smart, everyone thought he was dead, so why not stay that way? Son of a bitch."

Johnny held up a hand with his index finger extended.

"This stays in this room. No one else needs to know that bastard is still out there, and if we don't bother him, he won't bother us, which is fine by me. The man is a wrecking ball and we have enough damage to fix. The Conglomerate is on life support and it's a goddamn miracle we were able to hide the slaughter that Richards caused."

"How's that work?" Sophia said. "I mean, some of the men who died are big names in business, they can't just disappear."

"Accidents," Pullo said. "Lots of accidents, and it will look odd, so many at once, but it will cover things up here and in Europe."

"Like you did with Richards, making it look like his car went into the Hudson River?"

"Yeah, and the homicide cops might sniff around, but since no body was recovered, it will be classified as an accident and he'll be listed as Missing, Presumed Dead."

Johnny rubbed his chin and looked over at Sophia.

"Before your father died, did he get in a fight? Something with a knife maybe?"

"No, not that I know of, why?"

"Gino Tonti stabbed Tanner in the left leg a day before Gruber died. When I checked the body I thought was Tanner's, there was a wound on the left leg, a knife wound, or at least it looked like one."

Sophia's eyes grew wide with comprehension and she lowered her head to hide a grin, as she realized why Romeo was so secretive.

"Lots of wounds look like knife wounds," Sophia said. "Even a knitting needle might have made the mark."

Johnny stood, and the others followed.

Both Johnny and Pullo kissed Sophia on the cheek, and she left the office with a smile playing at the corners of her mouth.

Pullo gestured toward a handwritten letter on Johnny's desk.

"Is that from Mario?"

"Yeah, like I told you, he took the blame for everything and got his daughter off the hook. It's a damn shame that he did what he did, but he was a stand-up guy until the end."

They walked out into the club, nodded to Carl, who was restocking the glass shelves behind the bar, and walked outside.

"Can I give you a lift, Joe?"

Johnny pointed toward the new limo, where his new drivers awaited instruction.

Merle and Earl, both dressed in black suits and wearing chauffeur caps, looked busy as they used rags to polish the car.

Pullo threw his chin toward the boys. "What about the money they were paid as a reward for killing Tanner?"

"That bounty came from Richards' pockets, but we were to pay him back. Now that he's dead, it didn't cost us a cent, so what the hell, let them keep it. They probably blew it all by now anyway."

"I know you need a new driver, but why both of them?"

"They're a matched set and it's about the only thing they're good for."

Pullo smiled. "They're okay, and yeah, I will take a lift. I was going to drop in and see how Mario's daughter is doing."

Johnny sighed. "I'll go with you."

Merle and Earl leapt into action and soon the limo was on its way through the bustling city streets.

"Where do you think Tanner has gone to?" Johnny asked.

Before answering, Pullo thought of Laurel, and remembered her telling him that she loved Tanner.

"I don't know where he is, but I sure as hell hope he stays there."

∼

JOHNNY HAD TOLD SARA THE TRUE STORY OF RICHARDS' DEATH so that she might have peace, and she learned that the man she sought, Al Trent, had died as well, under mysterious circumstances in rural Pennsylvania.

Johnny hadn't told her that Tanner was still alive, for fear that she would go on a quest to find Tanner and kill him. He didn't care if Tanner lived or died, but he wanted to be with Sara and not share her with an obsession, or risk losing her at Tanner's hands.

~

Sara was in her living room, gazing out at the sky that lay beyond her balcony doors. She had been reading the morning paper but became lost in thought.

Richards was dead, Tanner was dead, and there was no longer anyone for her to pursue in her quest to avenge Brian Ames.

She had a new lover now, Johnny Rossetti, and a new future to create. Still, she felt restless, somehow empty. She wondered if she had subsisted on hate for so long that she'd forgotten how to live, and that life could offer more.

She had been spending time at Street View and enjoyed the investigative work of a reporter. She had learned much about Al Trent in the short time she had been searching for him and found his death a puzzle.

Sara tossed the newspaper account of Trent's death aside and rose to get dressed. Life awaited, and she wanted to see what came next.

~

FOUR HOURS LATER

Tanner was saying goodbye to Tim and Madison as they prepared to leave the farm.

Madison still wore a wide bandage on her forehead to cover the scrape she received when she hit her head against the tree, while Tim was wearing a walking boot for his ankle, which had suffered a grade-1 sprain when he tripped.

They were all out on the front porch, and Madison was trying to get the dog to come to her, but the shy hound kept her distance, despite wagging her tail.

"She saved our lives by barking," Tim said.

Madison frowned. "I'm worried about her, who will feed her now that we're all leaving?"

"She'll feed herself," Tanner said. "I saw her tearing into a possum this morning while I was out running."

Tanner's hair was dark again and the tattoos removed.

Romeo was no more.

With the files decoded, Tanner could return to Manhattan and use the information as a bargaining chip.

However, he had decided against it, at least for the time being, and was looking forward to moving on. He needed to go somewhere, somewhere where thoughts of Laurel Ivy didn't invade his mind. If he never saw her again, he felt he would forget her in time.

At least, he hoped so.

Ironically, now that Tim had the leverage to stop the attempts on his life, the man who wanted him dead was gone. The funds he had stolen had come from the electronic coffers of one of Frank Richards' companies, and with Richards dead and the rest of The Conglomerate in shambles, it was likely that no one would come looking for Tim again.

Tim had also entered their system and erased all traces of his crime. However, Johnny Rossetti knew of him, so Tim would make certain that the mob understood he could hurt them if they attempted retribution.

Still, Tim and Madison were free to live without fear for the first time since meeting, and like Tanner, they would start anew.

The rain remained and had been falling for days, as the storm system seemed to hover above the region. There were trees down all over the area, as the ground grew too soft to contain their roots and the lawn in front of the farmhouse had begun to resemble a rice paddy.

Tim gave Tanner's hand a firm shake, while Madison kissed him on the cheek, before locking eyes with him and nodding.

Tanner understood the meaning behind the nod. It was a

sign of both understanding and forgiveness for his having killed her father.

Any trace of love and affection that Madison had felt toward Frank Richards had left her when she realized that her father had sent people to murder her. Madison didn't blame Tanner in the slightest for what he had done.

The young couple drove off to start a new life, as thunder serenaded them and lightning lit their way.

Tanner was leaving as well and had packed his things into a pickup truck.

The farm was up for sale again under an alias, and given its history, it might be years before Tim sold it. Tanner walked about the farmhouse for the final time, while making sure that nothing had been left or forgotten.

He had just opened the front door to leave when the sound began, more tone than beep, and coming from somewhere within the house.

His weapons were packed away in the pickup truck, but of course, Tanner was armed. He carried a small gun, a Kimber Solo in a pocket holster, but he refrained from taking it out, as the noise wasn't ominous, just odd.

He found the source of the noise. It was a phone. Al Trent's phone. It had flown from Trent's hand and fallen behind the sofa after Tim had shot him.

Footsteps, soft, furtive, and when Tanner turned toward the doorway, he found Sara Blake standing there.

∼

FOUR HOURS EARLIER

Sara tossed the newspaper account of Trent's death aside and rose to get dressed for a new day. Life awaited, and she wanted to see what came next.

Her phone rang.

"Hello, Duke, what's up?"

"I got something new on Al Trent that I thought you might like to know."

"What could be new? The man is dead."

"True, but you know I like to be thorough, so I obtained a copy of Trent's belongings and discovered that his phone wasn't among his personal effects when he died."

Sara sat on the arm of her sofa.

"That is interesting. Who knows what could be on that phone."

"That was my thinking. You might also be interested to know that the other man found inside that overturned van was Gary Crasta. Crasta worked as a bodyguard for one Frank Richards. Maybe Richards is the reason the two of them were in Pennsylvania. I think they may have been setting up a place for Richards to go, you know, after he faked his death with a phony car crash."

Sara recalled what Johnny had told her. That a man named Romeo had killed Richards and that Johnny had disposed of the body and covered up the killing.

She nibbled at her bottom lip, as she pondered whether she could trust Johnny Rossetti. Was Richards dead, as Johnny claimed, or had he helped the man to fake his death and hide, and if so, why?

"Sara?"

"I'm here."

"What do you want to do?"

"I want to find that phone. I think you're right about it possibly containing information I could use, and if Richards is still alive, the phone may have been left at his location."

"I know a guy who could find it by hacking into one of those 'Find My Phone' services, but there's no guarantee that Trent had that option on his phone, or that the phone is even still on, but it might be worth a try."

It was, and four hours later, Sara found herself on Tim's farm.

She turned into the driveway with plans to park a short way in, so that she could walk the rest of the way and not reveal her presence.

When she made the turn into the driveway, a car driving behind her slowed, and for a moment, she thought it might be the homeowner returning. She cursed her timing, but the man at the wheel just drove on.

Sara locked her car and walked along the driveway while watching every step she took. Although the driveway had a gravel surface, the soil beneath it had turned to mud and made walking treacherous, as the stones beneath her feet shifted.

Meanwhile, the storm clouds thundered overhead, and the only thing louder was the incessant beating of the rain.

There was a pickup truck in front of the home, but she saw no lights on inside. Sara shifted her umbrella so that she could hold it in the crook of her arm and took out her tablet once more. She checked the location of Al Trent's phone by using the aerial map displayed on the App that tracked it.

Trent's phone was definitely inside the farmhouse. She activated the function that would make the phone emit a loud tone, thus, making its exact location easy to find.

Sara was ten feet from the porch when the door opened halfway.

She approached, thinking that someone would come out, but then she heard the sound of the tone, very faint from her position, but audible. She realized that whoever had opened the door must have gone to investigate the sound.

Maybe that someone is Frank Richards?

Sara went up the steps, peeked inside, and the sound grew clearer. As a precaution, she unsnapped her purse so that she had easy access to her gun. After laying the umbrella down, she crept into the home.

A man, not Richards, yet… somehow familiar, even from behind, and he was holding Al Trent's phone in his hand.

"Excuse me? I didn't mean to walk in on you, but the door was—oh my God… Tanner?"

Tanner blinked in surprise, dropped the phone, and went for his gun, even as Sara's hand disappeared into her purse.

They fired at the same instant.

One of them missed.

The other did not.

And death came to Forgotten Farm.

BONUS

THE FIRST THREE CHAPTERS OF BOOK FOUR – THE FIRST ONE TO DIE LOSES

51
THE GREATER OF TWO EVILS

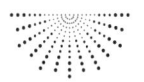

Tanner shook off his surprise at seeing Sara Blake at the farm and went for his gun.

He cleared the small pistol from his pocket in a smooth motion, while simultaneously thumbing off the safety. As he was doing this, he turned his body sideways to present a smaller target.

The gun was lined up with the center of Sara's forehead when Tanner became aware of the hulking figure coming up behind her and aiming a shotgun his way.

He made an instant adjustment in the angle of his shot and placed a round into the big man's chest. He was prepared to send his second shot at Sara, but was unable to, because when she returned fire, her shot had smashed into the front of his weapon and sent it flying from his hand.

That's when the big man collapsed onto Sara. The weight of his corpse drove her to the floor and trapped her legs beneath his bulk, as Tanner's shot had caught the man in the heart and killed him instantly.

Sara, having been unaware that the man was even there, cried out in shock, before angling her gun over her shoulder and firing off a second round.

The bullet entered the body beneath the left shoulder blade, but then Sara saw the man's empty eyes and knew that he was already dead.

She brought the gun back around to fire at Tanner and just caught a glimpse of him as he sped down a hallway headed for the rear of the house. She then spotted his gun, which was lying on the floor six feet away.

Her shot had rendered Tanner's weapon useless. Her bullet had hit the side of the barrel and knocked it askew, damaging the slide to such an extent that even the recoil spring could be glimpsed.

That meant that Tanner was unarmed and an easy kill, but when Sara tried to rise and go in pursuit, she realized that her legs were trapped beneath the dead man's bulk.

"Damn it!"

And as she struggled to free herself, she heard someone outside shout. That was followed by the sound of footsteps coming up the porch, as the rain continued to pour down in waves, and Tanner put distance between them.

~

WHEN TANNER AND SARA FIRED THEIR WEAPONS, OUTSIDE THE farmhouse Tyler Gray and Sherry Weston had looked at each other in dismay.

Tyler was a rawboned man who stood well over six feet tall and had stark cheekbones, along with an eyebrow ridge prominent enough to keep the rain out of his eyes.

Sherry was his lover, as well as his partner. She had dark hair and dark eyes, along with a wide mouth that was set in a permanent frown. Her body caused men to stare in desire and, at twenty-five, she was nine years younger than Tyler, and the more ruthless of the two. That was saying something, given Tyler's propensity toward violence.

The two of them had been standing beneath an evergreen

tree, while Tyler's younger brother, Randall, went to check out the house.

Just minutes earlier, they had been headed to the farmhouse when they saw Sara park in the driveway. After driving past and hanging a U-turn, they coasted their car to a stop behind Sara's.

Randall had been driving while Tyler and Sherry were in the back seat with the bags of money they'd stolen from a bank, in the nearby town of Ciderville.

Sherry's brow furrowed in confusion. "I thought the place was supposed to be abandoned?"

"It is, or it was, the damn place is called Forgotten Farm," Tyler said.

"Someone remembers it, or that woman wouldn't be here."

Randall tossed his chin in the direction of Sara's car. He was a huge man, as tall as Tyler, but bulky and not nearly as bright as his older brother.

"Why do you think she parked so far from the house?"

"Maybe it's too muddy up ahead, and that is a nice car," Tyler said.

Randall had grabbed his shotgun from the seat beside him and opened his door.

"I'll go check it out, Tyler."

"All right, but don't let the bitch see you until she opens the door, then find out how many are in the house. If it looks good, come get us and we'll take it over and have a place to hide until things calm down."

"Gotcha."

Randall took off at a trot, having no fear that Sara would hear his approach above the sound of the deluge that was pouring from the sky.

When Sara stopped to check something on the computer tablet she held, Randall had been less than a dozen steps behind her, and when she continued onward, he followed in her wake.

When the front door opened, Randall raised the shotgun, thinking that someone was coming out to greet the woman, but the door just stayed open partway. Sara went up the steps, while Randall stayed on the ground, standing behind the porch's railing.

After she discarded her umbrella, Randall followed Sara up the stairs, then caught sight of his brother and Sherry, as they took shelter beneath a tree on the side of the driveway.

They were both carrying a sack of money and had their guns out and at the ready.

Randall held up a hand, telling them to wait, then he entered the house with his shotgun up and his finger on the trigger.

Something inside the house was making an annoying sound, and the woman still hadn't realized he was behind her.

The sound seemed to perplex the woman, because she was creeping toward it. Randall had to slow his pace, or risk walking into her.

Up ahead in the living room, a man stood with his back to them and was holding the thing making all the noise, while staring down at it.

Then the woman spoke, the man spun around. The last sight that Randall ever saw was that of the man moving in a fluid deadly grace while firing a shot.

Randall's brain had just enough time to register the flash of the gun, before his heart exploded in his chest, and the world disappeared forever.

~

FIFTY-THREE MINUTES EARLIER

The armored car parked in front of the Fidelity Bank & Trust on Front Street in Ciderville and two armed guards exited by the rear door of the vehicle. They then walked into the bank carrying canvas bags that appeared to hold rolled coins.

The bags did not hold rolled coins; the guards, a man and a woman, were not really guards; and even the armored car was just a panel truck, which had been modified and painted to look as if it were from the armored car service the bank routinely employed.

The only thing real about them were their guns.

Tyler answered the welcoming smile of the armed bank guard by slamming the canvas bag into the side of his head. After the man fell to the ground looking dazed, Tyler snatched the gun from the man's holster and dumped out the rocks that the bag held.

Afterwards, he followed Sherry toward the bank manager's desk, while demanding that everyone, "Get down on the damn floor, now!"

The customers complied, as did the tellers, who disappeared behind their bullet-resistant glass. Tyler and Sherry weren't worried about a teller activating a silent alarm. They expected it, but also knew the average response time of the Ciderville Police, and they planned to be gone before they arrived.

Besides that, they had also phoned in a phony report of gunfire, which would have the police scrambling in the wrong direction.

The bank manager was a portly man with thinning brown hair and bright blue eyes. Tyler placed the tip of his gun between those eyes and made a demand.

"Take me to the vault."

The man did as ordered, while walking on shaky legs and, within two minutes, Tyler had the coin sacks filled with unmarked bills, while Sherry kept her gun aimed at the bank's patrons, one of whom kept staring up at her face, which was half-hidden beneath the oversized guard's cap she wore.

"What the hell are you looking at?"

The man didn't answer her, but he also didn't take his eyes off her.

Tyler returned seconds later and passed one of the sacks to

her. Sherry took it and looked back at the man in the suit who had been watching her.

She locked eyes with him, raised her gun, and placed a bullet in the center of his forehead. The scrutinizing gaze was no more.

Tyler spun around, saw what she had done, and let out a curse. Several women screamed and began crying, while an older man gripped a silver cross hanging around his neck and recited a prayer.

"Why did you shoot him?"

"He stared too much for his own good."

They left the bank, climbed into the phony armored car, and Randall drove them away.

The man Sherry murdered was named Michael Ryder. Killing him was the biggest mistake of her life.

52

MAN ON THE RUN

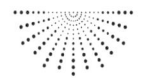

Tyler stared at the farmhouse "That wasn't a shotgun. Somebody's shooting at Randall."

Sherry thumbed off the safety on her gun. "Two people, I heard three shots from two different guns."

They moved out from under the tree. Tyler was faster and was nearly at the steps when Sherry spotted Tanner coming around the side of the house.

She yelled, "Hey!" and Tanner stopped moving and stared at her. When he spotted the gun in her hand, he reversed course, and headed for the trees behind the barn. He kept changing direction while he ran, to make himself harder to hit.

Sherry was about to let loose a shot despite knowing it had little chance of finding its target, but then she heard Tyler yelling Randall's name.

She entered the house and saw Tyler diving back toward her as a shot rang out. Tyler had dropped his sack as he dove for cover, and stacks of unmarked bills spilled out onto the floor.

"What the hell is going on?"

Tyler answered Sherry in a voice filled with hate, as he rose to his feet.

"Randall's been shot, and the bitch just fired at me too."

Sherry looked over and saw the soles of Randall's boots, and the movement of his body.

"He's alive, Tyler. I saw him move."

"It's her; Randall fell on top of her after she shot him."

Sara called out to them. "I didn't kill him. He was shot by a man named Tanner, and he's getting away."

"He's dead? My brother's dead?"

"Yes, I'm sorry, but yes."

"Why did you kill him?" Tyler said.

"I didn't, Tanner did, but I'll shoot you if you come any closer."

Sherry grabbed Tyler's arm. "She's not lying. I saw a man run into the trees in the back, um, dark hair, jeans, and a black hoodie."

Tyler pointed toward the living room. "I'll go get the motherfucker; you handle that bitch."

"No Tyler, first her, then him."

Tyler spoke as he ran out the door. "Just handle her and see to Randall. This bastard is not getting away."

Sherry cursed, but she moved toward the doorway to get a look at Sara. She eased her head around the doorframe just in time to see Sara free herself from beneath Randall's bulk.

"Don't move!"

Sara answered Sherry's demand by firing upwards at her. The shot missed by a foot, but it did cause Sherry to pull her head back. When she looked again, she saw that Sara was gone, but heard her footsteps as she fled down the hallway.

Sherry entered the room, knelt beside Randall as if to check for a pulse, but then saw the sightless eyes staring back at her.

"Oh shit. Shit! Shit! Shit!"

Sherry left the farmhouse in pursuit of Sara, amidst the driving rain. In the distance, there came the roar of Tyler's Magnum, causing Sherry to wonder if the dark-haired man had just been blown to bits.

53
SCARED RABBIT

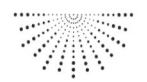

W‍ITH HIS GUN RENDERED USELESS AND HIS HAND STINGING IN pain, Tanner left the farmhouse by the back door, while his destination had been the pickup truck parked out front, where he could get a fresh weapon.

He barely had time to wonder at Sara's appearance on the farm, when he saw the woman headed for the porch. She carried a gun in her right hand and a money sack in her left.

Other than a pronounced frown, her face was indiscernible beneath the floppy rain hat she wore, but her shapely body and lithe movement spoke of her youth.

Tanner halted in his tracks, knowing he'd never make it to the pickup truck, then darted for the cover of the trees instead.

A man's voice came from inside the house, which sounded as if it were calling someone's name, but with the rain drumming in his ears, Tanner couldn't make it out.

The same could not be said for the gunshot that followed, which could be heard clearly, and Tanner realized that the man and woman must not be working with Sara Blake, but that they were a separate thing altogether.

Whatever it was, it was dangerous, and with his gun ruined by Sara's shot, he had only a knife for a weapon. That thought made him pause and he moved back toward the house until he could see it again.

The woman was no longer there and had likely gone inside.

Tanner estimated that he could reach his pickup truck in less than ten seconds and be armed again in fewer than twenty.

He was lurching forward to sprint toward the truck when the tall man came leaping off the side of the porch.

The man landed in a skid, because of the slickness of the grass, but righted himself quickly and headed toward Tanner's position. There was a gun in the man's hand, a huge revolver with a long barrel. Tanner turned and ran deeper into the trees before the man could spot him.

The ground was soggy even beneath the canopy of leaves overhead, as the series of small streams running through the forest had all overflowed. Water was also flowing down from higher elevations, and although the hour was barely past noon, the sky was dark from the black clouds that filled it.

Tanner was moving well and hoped that he was gaining a safe distance between himself and the man who pursued him. That hope faded when a shot that sounded like the boom of a cannon roared, and a sapling to his right was shredded at the middle of its trunk, and fell over.

"I see you, motherfucker and I'm gonna kill you!"

Tanner glanced over his shoulder in time to see the man rising from the crouching position he had assumed to take aim and fire.

Taking the time to fire that shot had widened the gap between them and Tanner intended to widen it farther still.

He sprinted over the uneven ground, seeking to lose his pursuer, while wishing he had a weapon with which to stand his ground.

And as he ran, he damned Sara and knew that once he handled the crazed man at his back, he would have to find her and put her down, but not before he learned how she had found him.

It had something to do with the phone he had discovered behind the sofa, the one that had emitted the tone, but he had to know if others also knew he was alive. If so, that too would have to be addressed, and he'd been so close to leaving and starting over.

The gun boomed again, and the ground in front of him threw up dirt and leaves in his path.

Tanner grimaced. Running about like a scared rabbit was not his way, but neither was dying because of a bruised ego. He would run from the man, or rather from the man's gun, and he would live to make him regret the chase.

The trees ended where a swollen stream rushed along, and toward the right was a rise ahead that led to the abandoned building site.

Tanner climbed the hill. When he reached the crest and was silhouetted against the sky, he could sense the man sighting the gun on his back.

He dropped to lay flat in the mud just as the third shot boomed overhead, then he rolled down the hill, oblivious of the two pairs of young eyes watching his every move.

TANNER RETURNS!

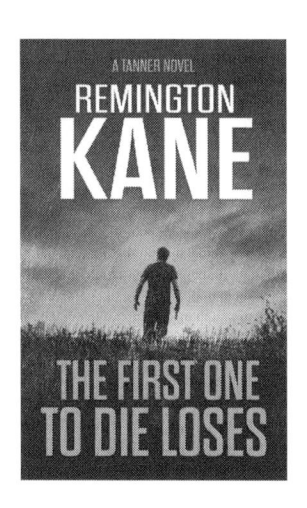

THE FIRST ONE TO DIE LOSES - BOOK 4

AFTERWORD

Thank you.

REMINGTON KANE

JOIN MY INNER CIRCLE

You'll receive FREE books, such as,

SLAY BELLS – A TANNER NOVEL – BOOK 0
    TAKEN! ALPHABET SERIES – 26 ORIGINAL TAKEN! TALES

Also – Exclusive short stories featuring TANNER, along with other books.

TO BECOME AN INNER CIRCLE MEMBER, GO TO:
    http://remingtonkane.com/mailing-list/

ALSO BY REMINGTON KANE

The TANNER Series in order

INEVITABLE I - A Tanner Novel - Book 1

KILL IN PLAIN SIGHT - A Tanner Novel - Book 2

MAKING A KILLING ON WALL STREET - A Tanner Novel - Book 3

THE FIRST ONE TO DIE LOSES - A Tanner Novel - Book 4

THE LIFE & DEATH OF CODY PARKER - A Tanner Novel - Book 5

WAR - A Tanner Novel - Book 6

SUICIDE OR DEATH - Book 7

TWO FOR THE KILL - Book 8

BALLET OF DEATH - Book 9

MORE DANGEROUS THAN MAN - Book 10

TANNER TIMES TWO - Book 11

OCCUPATION: DEATH - Book 12

HELL FOR HIRE - Book 13

A HOME TO DIE FOR - Book 14

FIRE WITH FIRE - Book 15

TO KILL A KILLER - Book 16

WHITE HELL – Book 17

MANHATTAN HIT MAN – Book 18

ONE HUNDRED YEARS OF TANNER – Book 19

REVELATIONS - Book 20

THE SPY GAME - Book 21

A VICTIM OF CIRCUMSTANCE - Book 22
A MAN OF RESPECT - Book 23
THE MAN, THE MYTH - Book 24
ALL-OUT WAR - Book 25
THE REAL DEAL - Book 26

The Young Guns Series in order

YOUNG GUNS
YOUNG GUNS 2 - SMOKE & MIRRORS
YOUNG GUNS 3 - BEYOND LIMITS
YOUNG GUNS 4 - RYKER'S RAIDERS
YOUNG GUNS 5 - ULTIMATE TRAINING
YOUNG GUNS 6 - CONTRACT TO KILL
YOUNG GUNS 7 - FIRST LOVE
YOUNG GUNS 8 - THE END OF THE BEGINNING

A Tanner Series in order

TANNER: YEAR ONE
TANNER: YEAR TWO

The TAKEN! Series in order

TAKEN! - LOVE CONQUERS ALL - Book 1
TAKEN! - SECRETS & LIES - Book 2
TAKEN! - STALKER - Book 3
TAKEN! - BREAKOUT! - Book 4
TAKEN! - THE THIRTY-NINE - Book 5
TAKEN! - KIDNAPPING THE DEVIL - Book 6

TAKEN! - HIT SQUAD - Book 7

TAKEN! - MASQUERADE - Book 8

TAKEN! - SERIOUS BUSINESS - Book 9

TAKEN! - THE COUPLE THAT SLAYS TOGETHER - Book 10

TAKEN! - PUT ASUNDER - Book 11

TAKEN! - LIKE BOND, ONLY BETTER - Book 12

TAKEN! - MEDIEVAL - Book 13

TAKEN! - RISEN! - Book 14

TAKEN! - VACATION - Book 15

TAKEN! - MICHAEL - Book 16

TAKEN! - BEDEVILED - Book 17

TAKEN! - INTENTIONAL ACTS OF VIOLENCE - Book 18

TAKEN! - THE KING OF KILLERS – Book 19

TAKEN! - NO MORE MR. NICE GUY - Book 20 & the Series Finale

The BLUE STEELE Series in order

BLUE STEELE - BOUNTY HUNTER- Book 1

BLUE STEELE - BROKEN- Book 2

BLUE STEELE - VENGEANCE- Book 3

BLUE STEELE - THAT WHICH DOESN'T KILL ME- Book 4

BLUE STEELE - ON THE HUNT- Book 5

BLUE STEELE - PAST SINS - Book 6

BLUE STEELE - DADDY'S GIRL - Book 7 & the Series Finale

The CALIBER DETECTIVE AGENCY Series in order

CALIBER DETECTIVE AGENCY - GENERATIONS- Book 1

CALIBER DETECTIVE AGENCY - TEMPTATION- Book 2

CALIBER DETECTIVE AGENCY - A RANSOM PAID IN BLOOD- Book 3

CALIBER DETECTIVE AGENCY - MISSING- Book 4

CALIBER DETECTIVE AGENCY - DECEPTION- Book 5

CALIBER DETECTIVE AGENCY - CRUCIBLE- Book 6

CALIBER DETECTIVE AGENCY – LEGENDARY – Book 7

CALIBER DETECTIVE AGENCY – WE ARE GATHERED HERE TODAY - Book 8

CALIBER DETECTIVE AGENCY - MEANS, MOTIVE, and OPPORTUNITY - Book 9 & the Series Finale

THE TAKEN!/TANNER Series in order

THE CONTRACT: KILL JESSICA WHITE - Taken!/Tanner - Book 1

UNFINISHED BUSINESS – Taken!/Tanner – Book 2

THE ABDUCTION OF THOMAS LAWSON - Taken!/Tanner – Book 3

DETECTIVE PIERCE Series in order

MONSTERS - A Detective Pierce Novel - Book 1

DEMONS - A Detective Pierce Novel - Book 2

ANGELS - A Detective Pierce Novel - Book 3

THE OCEAN BEACH ISLAND Series in order

THE MANY AND THE ONE - Book 1

SINS & SECOND CHANES - Book 2

DRY ADULTERY, WET AMBITION -Book 3

OF TONGUE AND PEN - Book 4

ALL GOOD THINGS… - Book 5

LITTLE WHITE SINS - Book 6
THE LIGHT OF DARKNESS - Book 7
STERN ISLAND - Book 8 & the Series Finale

THE REVENGE Series in order

JOHNNY REVENGE - The Revenge Series - Book 1
THE APPOINTMENT KILLER - The Revenge Series - Book 2
AN I FOR AN I - The Revenge Series - Book 3

ALSO

THE EFFECT: Reality is changing!
THE FIX-IT MAN: A Tale of True Love and Revenge
DOUBLE OR NOTHING
PARKER & KNIGHT
REDEMPTION: Someone's taken her
DESOLATION LAKE
TIME TRAVEL TALES & OTHER SHORT STORIES

MAKING A KILLING ON WALL STREET
Copyright © REMINGTON KANE, 2015
YEAR ZERO PUBLISHING

This book is a work of fiction. Names, characters, places and incidents either are products of the author's imagination or are used fictitiously.

Any resemblance to actual events or locales or persons, living or dead, is entirely coincidental.

All rights reserved. Except as permitted under the U.S. Copyright Act of 1976, no part of this publication may be reproduced, distributed or transmitted in any form or by any means, or stored in a database or retrieval system, without the prior written permission of the publisher.

❦ Created with Vellum

Printed in Great Britain
by Amazon